WRAITHS & WRITERS

A LIBRARY WITCH MYSTERY

ELLE ADAMS

This book was written, produced and edited in the UK, where some spelling, grammar and word usage will vary from US English.

Copyright © 2020 Elle Adams
All rights reserved.

To be notified when Elle Adams's next book is released, sign up to her author newsletter.

1

I turned the page of my late father's journal and prepared to read the translated document, hoping nobody would interrupt me this time around. A quiet morning might be too much to expect from a magical library inhabited by five people, three familiars, and more books than should logically have been able to fit into the space it occupied, but this stretch of time seemed promisingly quiet.

Time to unearth my dad's long-kept secrets.

Getting my hands on a translation of my dad's old journal entries had been a battle and a half already. Not only had I needed my Aunt Adelaide's code-breaker spell to figure out how to read the journal, but I'd also had to track down a specific document my dad had hidden in the bookshop he'd worked at during my childhood in order to actually use said code-breaker, since he'd invented his very own magical code to prevent anyone else from reading a word of it. Complicating matters was the fact that after he'd met my mum, he'd made the decision to turn his back on the magical world entirely, so I'd grown up with no clue that my dad had once lived among witches, wizards, werewolves, elves... and vampires.

The latter were the primary reason for my apprehension when I looked down at the first page, which was dated more than twenty years ago. I'd been a small child at the time, and it was strange to imagine my dad scribbling away in the journal while I'd been utterly unaware of the world he'd once belonged to.

I've been advised to write this in code. I think it's unnecessary, but that way, if the journal is found by the wrong people, they won't be able to make sense of it.

So I'm using a code which even the library I grew up in wouldn't be able to translate without access to the code-breaker document. Perhaps it's overkill, but it's easier this way. At least I can be certain Rory won't be dragged into this.

Reading my own name brought a pang to my chest. Whatever my dad had wanted to keep me safe from had eventually found its way to my doorstep in the form of a group of vampires who wanted to get their hands on the journal by any means possible. As a result, I'd been utterly unprepared for my sudden introduction to the paranormal world at the end of last year. Since then, I'd accepted that my dad had had a good reason for keeping secrets from me, but the vampires' taunts about my dad's history with them had wormed their way into my head. Specifically, their hints that he'd wanted to keep the magical world secret from me because there was something in his own history that he didn't want me to know about.

There was nothing to prove they were telling the truth or not except for this document in my hands, so it was no wonder I'd been apprehensive to read it, but it'd remained like a lead weight on my chest regardless of whether I read it or not. Better that I got it over with.

I turned back to the page. More words in my dad's cramped handwriting were scribbled in the margins, added at a later date. *I'm glad I did this. The Founders have got wind of what I'm doing, so I'm grateful that there's no way anyone can read this without access to the code-breaker document.*

My heart gave a jolt at the confirmation that the group of vampires known as the Founders had indeed been looking for my father long before he'd died. They'd all but hinted as much to me already. Mortimer Vale and his two friends were locked up in a secure prison, but the remainder of the group remained at large, and my dad had seemingly laid his hands on some kind of information they were willing to kill to possess. If I read the journal in its entirety, I'd potentially make myself a target the way my dad had. Yet the Founders had already come after me more than once, and as long as I remained ignorant of what they were looking for, I'd remain at a disadvantage.

I turned back to the page. Rustling sounded over my shoulder and I turned around to see a large tawny owl perched on the shelf behind me. "Don't mind me," he said. "Carry on with whatever you're doing."

I put down the journal. "This is private, Sylvester."

"Ooh." He ruffled his feathers as he peered over to read the page, and I swatted him on the beak.

"Cut it out," I told the owl. "Can you please go and bother someone else?"

Thanks, Sylvester. I should have guessed my family's cantankerous and nosy owl familiar would show up the instant I began to get some answers about my dad's mysterious history with the vampires.

He shuffled over to my shoulder. "It's more fun to bother you."

A small jet-black shape flew into view and landed next to the journal. Jet, my crow familiar, looked up at the owl from the desk. "Should I chase him off, partner?"

"He's welcome to try," said Sylvester.

Typical. After all the other disruptions I'd dealt with in the process of trying to get the journal translated, Sylvester's attention-seeking tendencies seemed minor, but that didn't mean I wanted a feathery battle to erupt above my head. The owl hated being ignored, and he wasn't a fan of most of the library's other inhabitants, either.

"No need, Jet." I slid the translated pages back into the journal and closed it firmly. "I'm done here."

"Good, because I need your help upstairs," said Sylvester. "That friend of yours is trying to get through one of the closed doors up on the first floor again."

"Why didn't you lead with that?" I beckoned the little crow over to me. "Can you fetch Estelle to watch the desk while I'm upstairs?"

"Of course, partner!" he squeaked.

While Jet took flight, I resigned myself to abandoning the journal for a bit. Shrugging my bag over my shoulder, I made for the curving staircase which linked all five stories. Towering shelves filled each floor behind wooden balconies, while the sun streamed through the stained-glass windows and bathed everything in golden light. The smell of old tomes and the faint sound of rustling pages pursued me up the staircase until I touched down on the first floor.

I wove through the towering shelves, following Sylvester's tawny form, until I found Laney standing nose to nose with a stretch of brick wall.

"I know you're a door," she told the wall. "You can't fool me. I saw you change into a wall just then."

I stepped up behind her. "Which section are you trying to get into?"

Laney whirled around, startling both of us. "Whoa. Sorry, Rory. Didn't hear you then."

I remained tensed, my heart hammering against my ribcage as I waited for my body to get the message that I wasn't being chased. "I thought you could hear things from a mile off."

"Yeah, that's the problem," she said. "I can hear everything in the entire library and it's distracting me. Every conversation, every small sound… it's hard for me to focus."

"Sorry." I breathed in and out, willing my heart rate to calm down. My best friend, Laney, was adjusting after our last encounter with Mortimer Vale and his vampire friends had left some permanent aftereffects. She'd mostly taken her transformation into a vampire in stride, but she was having trouble with some of her newfound talents. As a result, she tended to hang out in the areas of the library which weren't as crowded so her newly enhanced senses and mind-reading abilities didn't overwhelm her.

"It's not your fault," she said. "Anyway, can you open this door?"

"Are you sure it's a door?" I examined the flat bricks,

seeing no signs of a door handle or anything else. "Which section were you trying to get into, anyway?"

"I thought it was the Vampire Section," she said. "I wanted to look up more about my condition."

"Nah, this isn't the Vampire Section." I stepped away from the wall. "C'mon, we'll find it."

I'd lost sight of Sylvester, but it didn't particularly surprise me that he'd got bored and flown off. The owl wasn't exactly what you'd call reliable, except when it came to matters such as disturbing me when I was in the middle of trying to read my dad's journal.

Laney and I wove through the towering shelves until we came to the right area, but the door didn't appear in its usual spot. Nothing was a hundred percent constant when it came to the library, but I'd memorised the location of this particular door after the amount of time I'd had to spend looking up information on our fanged companions in the last few weeks.

"Don't tell me Cass rearranged things again." I was willing to bet it was either Cass or Sylvester who was responsible, since both were prone to playing practical jokes and neither of them had taken to our new guest.

Laney rolled her eyes. "Okay, I won't tell you."

Just as well that nothing fazed Laney. Not even being undead, or my misanthropic cousin. She glided away from the wall with much more grace then she'd had as a human. I could never quite describe how vampires walked, any more than I could quite put my finger on the way she'd changed. Her face was paler, ethereal, her hair glossier, and her movements graceful as a ballet dancer. Yet underneath all that, she was still Laney.

It sometimes seemed as though the guilt over her

predicament would never quite leave me. I'd wanted to introduce my best friend to the magical world ever since I'd first moved here to the library, but on the surface, it'd seemed like an impossible dream. Humans weren't allowed to be part of the paranormal world, and my dad had adhered to those rules so strictly that I'd grown up without a clue I was magical at all. When Laney had found her way into my life anyway, I'd been thrilled.

Yet it'd turned out to be too good to be true. The Founders had targeted her, which had resulted in her getting a crash-course in magic. Fuelled by vampire blood she'd drunk at one of their events, she'd attempted to take out the vampires hunting me down with her own hands. In the end, she'd wound up being bitten herself, losing her humanity in the process. After undergoing a painful transformation, she'd come to live here in the library with my family, and we were still figuring out where to go from there.

I examined the spot where the door ought to have been. "Nope, it's gone. It'll be back soon, I don't doubt. I'm glad you didn't end up stuck in there with the book wraith, anyway."

"I can handle a book wraith." She turned away from the wall with the same graceful movements as before. "All right, I'll come back later."

We crossed the first floor, hearing footsteps from somewhere above. When we reached the staircase, Cass came into view, heading down from the second floor, where she kept a number of animals which she liked considerably more than the rest of us. *There was also a good chance she was responsible for the missing door.* Since Cass didn't like people in general, she'd been less than impressed when a normal had showed up in the library, much less when she'd ended up turning into a vampire and having to stay here as a result. It'd taken Cass long enough to accept that *I'd* be staying here in the library for the long-term, let alone this new development.

Laney tensed behind me at the sight of my cousin. While her transformation into a vampire had caused them to come to a temporary truce, I'd often caught them glaring at one another, and a constant low-level tension simmered underneath the surface. Unlike me, Laney wasn't Cass's relation, so I didn't know what more she could do to prove she wasn't a threat to Cass or the library. While my own induction to the magical world had got off to a rocky start, I'd ended up settling in well and even had my dad's old wand to prove my legitimacy. While Cass and I didn't see eye to eye on a lot of things—including my decision to date the Grim Reaper's apprentice, Xavier—she'd developed a grudging respect for me which might even turn into friendship later down the line.

Laney, though, wasn't even officially working in the library yet, while she hadn't met most of the town's citizens. She'd wanted to make sure she had her bloodlust under control before venturing outside the library. As a result, Cass was forced into proximity with her whether she liked it or not.

I caught up to Cass as she breezed past me. Her red hair was twisted into a topknot, her glasses and cloak sprinkled with sawdust, and a book was tucked underneath her arm.

"Did you rearrange the doors?" I asked her. "On the first floor? The Vampire Section has wandered off."

Cass gave me a brief look. "Why would I bother doing that?"

"Sylvester did it, then," I said. "He's in one of his annoying moods today."

We reached the lowest floor again, where a number of patrons gathered in the Reading Corner at the back. Plush sofas, bean bags and chairs were nestled between the shelves, while several tables formed a studying area for students from the local academy and university. I didn't blame Laney for seeking higher ground to get away from the noise.

We made our way to the front desk to find Estelle clearing away a pile of books. She shared our family's trademark red hair, though hers was loose and she was shorter and curvier than Cass was. Spark the pixie fluttered overhead, making chattering noises. I couldn't understand a word he said, but Estelle had been making an effort to learn his language so they could communicate with one another. The pixie was yet another source of annoyance to Cass, who'd made no shortage of complaints about him dropping glitter on everything in sight.

"Hey, Rory," Estelle said. "And you too, Laney. No problems?"

"Not at all," said Laney, with a glare at Cass. "I can hear your thoughts, you know. I don't appreciate you broadcasting your insults at me. It's getting old."

Cass scoffed. "Shouldn't nose around in my head, then. You might not like what you find in there."

"That's enough," said Estelle. "Cass, can you at least try not to be antagonistic?"

"We never discussed keeping a long-term guest in here

amongst ourselves as a family," said Cass. "You just assumed we all agreed with you."

"Yes, we did discuss it," I said. "And you were outvoted. Laney isn't going anywhere."

"Damn right I'm not," Laney said. "Where's that vampire book of yours?"

"Over here." I moved to the desk and hunted for the *Vampire Defence* book, which had been instrumental in helping Laney adjust to the change without the aid of the other vampires. I then handed the book to Laney, suppressing the urge to give Cass a stern talking-to. It wouldn't do any good, not as long as the source of her irritation was still here. Besides, Laney herself wasn't exactly helping matters by exercising her mind-reading skills whenever Cass got too close to her.

In a way, I understood Cass's annoyance, given her general aversion to strangers, but Laney had nowhere else to stay. Her mind-reading powers made it hard for her to handle large crowds… and that wasn't even getting into her newly acquired thirst for human blood.

Despite all the bumps in the road we'd faced, I had to admit it was nice to be in the same place as my best friend again, while I no longer had to worry about keeping my new life hidden from the person I trusted the most. As a bonus, spending so much time around Laney had gone a long way to helping me begin to move past the fear of vampires which had pursued me ever since my induction to the magical world.

Estelle eyed the book in Laney's hands. "Are you sure you need self-defence classes? Didn't you knock a bookshelf onto Cass the other day when she startled you?"

"That was an accident," she said. "Anyway, it's Rory who wanted to practise."

Laney and I had begun taking our magical theory classes together, since we were both new to the magical world and my own knowledge didn't go much further than hers. Practical lessons were harder, because while she was happy to act as a dummy for me to practise spells on, I had zero desire to become a human pincushion while she refined her blood-drinking technique. As for mind-reading, she had yet to master the art of focusing for long enough to intentionally read someone's thoughts, which was probably a good thing.

"Which spell are you on now?" asked Estelle.

"Locking and unlocking spells," I said. "Last time I locked myself in the vampire's basement and then couldn't get out, so we need a little more practise."

After the recent upheavals in my life, the focus of my magical lessons had revolved around learning to defend myself. Locking myself in the basement with the library's resident sleeping vampire had not been on my plan, though.

"How are you doing with duelling spells?" asked Estelle.

"I can conjure up a shield, but I still drop it whenever there's a sudden movement." Which was not helpful when I was faced with any vampires, who were incapable of *not* being startlingly fast.

"You're doing great," said Estelle. "Honestly, a lot of veteran witches and wizards struggle with practical magic. It's not like we're built for combat—Cass, what are you doing?"

"What?" Cass had begun to walk back towards the

stairs, as though she had every intention of hiding with her animals again.

"I thought you were going to help with the returns." Estelle indicated the towering pile beside the front desk.

Cass glanced over her shoulder. "I don't see you falling over yourself to ask your new friend to help you out."

"Cass." I blew out a frustrated breath. "Why did you even come down here if you're just going to be obnoxious?"

"She's thinking about getting a unicorn next," Laney supplied.

Cass went brick red. "Get *out* of my head."

"Wait!" Estelle protested, but Cass was already marching away, her cloak streaming behind her.

I rolled my eyes after her, and then turned to Laney. "Really?"

"She asked for it," said Laney. "Besides, do you really want a unicorn in here?"

Aunt Adelaide bustled into view. "Oh, there you are, Rory, Estelle. Have you seen Candace?"

"No." Like Estelle, my aunt had the family's signature red hair, and a curvier figure than her sister. She wore the same uniform as all of us: a silver-lined black cloak embossed with our family symbol, which consisted of a pair of wands crossed above an owl sitting atop an open book.

Estelle moved over to the pile of returns. "Why, is she not working on her book?"

"She isn't in her room," said her mother. "I wondered if she went out."

"She might have." Of all of us, Aunt Candace left the library the least often and only on special occasions, but that didn't mean I had the slightest idea what she might be up to this time. With Aunt Candace, I was usually better off not knowing.

"Yeah, she probably went to get some air. Or inspiration." Estelle waved her wand and moved some of the books from the return pile into a separate stack on the desk. "Right, we really need to deal with these returns. I'll divide them up by floor."

"That works," I said. "Laney and I can do the first floor. Then we can look for that door again. The Vampire Section has moved somewhere. We couldn't find it earlier."

"Seriously?" she said. "Well, that's annoying."

"It's okay, I have this," said Laney, waving the *Vampire Defence* book I'd given her. "If Cass wants to keep screwing around with the doors, I'll wait until later."

"I think it was Sylvester, actually," I said. "He's the one who told me you were stuck. If he keeps showing up to pester me whenever I have a moment's peace, at this rate I'll be lucky to finish reading my dad's journal at the end of the century."

Between dealing with the library and its many inhabitants, not to mention my ongoing lessons in magic, the odds of sneaking a quiet moment were low enough already. Still, I couldn't complain about having a boring life.

"I'll have a word with him," said Aunt Adelaide. "Ah—there she is."

Aunt Candace came sailing into the library, her cloak billowing behind her and her hair windswept. "I have great news."

"Oh?" I said warily. To Aunt Candace, good news

either consisted of an idea for her next book, or some kind of research opportunity, some of which had ended badly. Like when she'd got herself locked in jail and driven the police out of their minds by bombarding them with questions. Oh, and the time when she'd scored us all invitations to a party at the vampires' home which had ended with someone being murdered. Admittedly, that part wasn't actually her fault, but trouble followed her consistently wherever she went. If anything, she welcomed it.

"No need to look so frightened," she said. "Where are the others? They'll want to hear this."

"Hear what?" Aunt Adelaide asked her sister. "The only person not here is Cass."

"And I doubt she'd care either way," I added.

"You've got that right," Cass's voice drifted down from the direction of the stairs.

Aunt Candace tutted. "You never fail to disappoint. This is the best news I've had in a long time."

"Go on, tell us," said Aunt Adelaide.

"I've been nominated for an award," Aunt Candace announced. "Or to be more accurate, my alter ego has."

"Which one?" I asked. Aunt Candace had a pen name for every day of the week.

"My mystery pen name, Zora Martine," she said. "I've been shortlisted for the Merry Mysteries award."

At least it wasn't for the book based on my dad's life story. That was a bit too personal for my liking.

"Well done," said Estelle, and the rest of us chimed in agreement.

"So when does the winner get announced?" asked Aunt Adelaide.

"There will be an award ceremony," she said, "and the library has been nominated as one of the possible venues. It's a great honour for all of us."

"By nominated, do you mean *you* put it forward?" I turned to Aunt Adelaide, who wore an expression which suggested she'd come to the same conclusion as I had. She was usually the one whose permission we had to ask before using the library to host an event. Even Estelle, head of social events, deferred to her mother when it came to this sort of thing. Especially any events which involved Aunt Candace.

"Are they likely to choose the library as the venue?" said Aunt Adelaide.

"Maybe," said Aunt Candace. "I think it would be great for us. A new way to bring more tourism to the town. There'll be dozens of people attending the ceremony."

Estelle's mouth pressed together. "I suppose our tourism industry is in need of a boost. There's not much else going on at this time of year."

"The library has enough guest rooms for all the nominees, doesn't it?" said Aunt Candace. "The other venues are hotels, but I'm sure the library can be an effective substitute."

"I don't know," said Aunt Adelaide. "We've never had that number of guests in here before, much less overnight."

"There aren't that many shortlisted nominees," said Aunt Candace. "Besides, it'll be good for the library's reputation."

Estelle's back straightened, her eyes brightening. I could see the thoughts ticking over in her mind. "I suppose."

"I'll also be unmasking my pen name," she added. "So that'll be worth watching."

"Um, Aunt Candace, I'm pretty sure people will figure out your identity when you invite them to the library," said Estelle. "Considering we're the only ones who live here. And the library is well-known enough that they'll make the connection."

"It's the principle of the thing," she said. "I've kept this name a secret for years."

"Except from us," said Cass, sauntering into view. "And Edwin. And half the students at the academy. Oh, and Zee at the bakery—"

"You've made your point," said Aunt Candace. "Anyway, it shouldn't take much preparation to get the library ready. We've done events like this before, haven't we?"

"We have," said Estelle. "I can handle that side of things, no problem."

"If you're sure," said Aunt Adelaide. "We don't have anything else going on for the next few months, at least until the weather improves."

"Precisely," said Aunt Candace.

Cass gave an eye-roll. "Have you ever noticed that when we *do* have things going on, it ends up being more trouble than it's worth?"

"It's only an award ceremony," said Aunt Candace. "Really. I thought you'd be happy."

"I am," said Estelle. "Just trying to figure out the logistics. When is it?"

"One week from Friday. Is that enough time to plan?"

"It is." We all knew Estelle could pull together a great event at a moment's notice, given the chance. She'd done it before.

The slight issue? We hadn't held an event bigger than the weekly poetry night since Laney had come to live here in the library. We certainly hadn't had other guests staying overnight either.

"Okay," said Aunt Adelaide. "We'll put the library forward as one of the contenders for the venue. If we win, we'll deal with that when it comes to it."

I hoped it'd be that simple. When I looked at Laney, I saw wariness in her expression, and a flutter of unease stirred within me.

If she was having difficulty being around individual people, how would she cope with a huge event with a bunch of strangers?

2

"We won," Aunt Candace said triumphantly, first thing the following morning. "I knew we would. We're the best venue in town, and I made sure they all knew it."

"Are you sure you didn't influence the decision process?" said Aunt Adelaide.

Aunt Candace made a shocked noise. "I can't believe you'd accuse me, your own sister, of doing such a thing."

"Did you, though?"

"It was the right choice," she said. "The other options were a golf course and an old castle in the middle of nowhere."

"A castle would be cool," said Estelle.

"It's too far away from the library," said Aunt Candace. "I wanted to be able to work on my manuscript without being interrupted."

"You're assuming Sylvester won't start singing in your ear every time you try to write as payback for disrupting his peace and quiet, aren't you?" I pointed out.

Aunt Candace scowled.

The guests were due to arrive on Friday, so we had less than a week to get the library ready. At least we had magic to make the job easier, though the library itself was impossible to tame entirely. Between the vanishing corridors, moving doors, invisible stairs and other oddities, we'd be lucky to stop anything from going sideways for five minutes, much less a full weekend.

Shockingly, I made little progress on translating my dad's journal while the preparations were in progress. Every time I sat down to open my notes, my aunts or cousins needed my help with something. Laney wanted to help out, but often had to stand on the side due to her relative unfamiliarity with the library's magic. I could tell she was getting nervous about our impending visitors, too, since she'd been dipping into our newly acquired blood stores more frequently than before. Admittedly, she'd managed to refrain from biting anyone so far, but that might well change when a bunch of Aunt Candace's eccentric acquaintances descended on the library. I didn't blame her for worrying, considering the other guest rooms were a mere staircase away from her own quarters, and if anyone found out we had a resident vampire, expecting them to restrain their curiosity might be too much to ask.

The day of the event rolled around, and I woke up early when someone rapped on my bedroom door.

"Who is it?" I yawned.

"It's me," said Aunt Adelaide. "Come downstairs as soon as you can. The guests are already arriving."

I checked the time. It was barely eight in the morning. Who could possibly already be here at this hour? They must have left at the crack of dawn to get to Ivory Beach so early. Yawning, I hurriedly dressed and grabbed my shoulder bag, and then went downstairs to find my aunts in conversation in the entryway to our family's living quarters.

"What's going on?" I said. "Who showed up this early? Did they get the time wrong?"

"Betsy Blake," said Aunt Candace. "She always has to be first for everything."

"Estelle is with her in the lobby," Aunt Adelaide said. "The guest rooms aren't ready yet, and the library isn't even supposed to be open until nine. Besides, I wanted to give the place a last check for potential issues before I let anyone in."

"I can help stall her," I said. "She can wait in the Reading Corner until the rooms are ready, right?"

"Thanks, Rory," said Aunt Adelaide distractedly. "I'll come and speak to her when I've figured out where that owl has gone. If I find him in another guest's room…"

"What are you doing, Aunt Candace?" I asked, as my other aunt shuffled past me down the corridor. "We need your help."

"I can't possibly greet the guests until I've had my coffee," she said. "Trust me, they don't want to meet me pre-caffeine."

She probably wasn't wrong on that one. "All right, but don't sneak upstairs to write your book. We need you down here."

I hadn't had the chance to grab any coffee for myself, but I'd prefer not to leave Estelle to handle the guests alone and I needed to make sure Laney wasn't taken by surprise, too. I entered the lobby to find Estelle talking to a woman with a lot of blond hair coiled atop her head in a way that resembled a python. She wore what appeared to be a cape and a pair of matching trousers in a violent shade of purple, while her face glowed all over with what was presumably some kind of beauty enhancement spell.

"Hey," I said to the newcomer. "I'm Rory. Estelle's cousin."

"Candace's niece… the lost cousin?" Her eyes widened. "Wow. It's an honour to meet you."

Her awed tone brought a flush to my cheeks. It sometimes surprised me how far the 'lost cousin' story had spread, especially when Aunt Candace's pen names were supposed to be a secret to most people. "That's me. Are you one of the nominees for the Merry Mysteries prize?"

"I am," she said. "I'm Betsy Blake, and I'm a bestselling mystery author. Is your aunt here?"

"She's just getting your room ready for you." *Or getting caffeinated.* "Want to come to the Reading Corner? You can wait there for the others to arrive."

Estelle shot me a grateful look as I led Betsy to the Reading Corner at the back, which we'd universally voted on as the safest place to leave the guests unattended with minimal risk of trouble. We wouldn't properly transform the lobby for the ceremony until the evening when all the patrons had gone home and only the guests remained. With one eye on the ceiling in case Sylvester decided to show his face unexpectedly, I gave our guest an abbreviated tour of the ground floor.

"Nice place, this." Betsy took in the plush chairs, soft beanbags and hammocks, surrounded by tall shelves heaving with books. "I can see where Candace gets her ideas from. I suppose she doesn't need to make anything up if she lives in a place like this. Does she often base events in her books on real life?"

"Occasionally," I said delicately, knowing Aunt Candace wouldn't want us gossiping about her work behind her back.

"Thought so," she said. "I've read these sorts of mysteries for years, so I was well prepared to write one of my own. I read your aunt's books and decided that if it was so easy for her to do it, then I would have no trouble whatsoever. Turns out I was right. Imagine that!"

"Uh-huh." I made a mental note to keep Aunt Candace away from her corner, caffeinated or otherwise, and politely extricated myself from the conversation. "I have to go and open the library for the patrons, but feel free to let one of us know if you need anything. Also, you can read any of the books in this section while you wait for the others to show up."

The Reading Corner contained mostly fiction and was relatively safe, but that didn't mean I entirely trusted our new guest. As I turned away, I called my familiar, who flew down to land on my palm.

"Jet," I said to the little crow, "can you watch over Betsy in the Reading Corner to make sure she doesn't get into trouble?"

"Of course, partner!" He fluttered up to perch on the hammock hanging in the middle of the Reading Corner, while I went back to the front desk to join Estelle.

"Hope it's a quiet day," I said to her. "I'm starting to wish we'd closed the place to regular patrons until the event's done."

"Yeah, I didn't expect anyone to show up before nine," she said. "It's okay, though. We can handle one person."

"Not sure Aunt Candace can, given the way she was talking about her books." Still, I'd expected some level of professional jealousy among the guests, given that they were directly competing against one another for the award. "I'm gonna grab some coffee before we open. Want some?"

"Sure." She smiled. "Thanks."

After a hasty dash to the kitchen to grab breakfast and coffee, we set about opening the library for the day. As luck would have it, the instant the clocks struck nine o'clock, the door opened and a pack of students sailed into the library, talking loudly among themselves. I didn't get a free moment to check up on Betsy Blake until after Estelle and I had helped the students find the various books they needed, and by that point, she'd made herself at home in the Reading Corner, where she was giving the patrons loud lectures on the techniques for plotting a mystery.

Figuring that at least she was staying in one place and not roaming around the library, I left her to it and got on with helping the patrons find the books they were looking for.

Aunt Candace finally showed her face when I slipped away in a quiet moment to see if Laney was up yet.

"There you are," I said to Aunt Candace, as she walked out of our living quarters and into the lobby. "Where have you been?"

"I was getting my outfit ready for the ceremony," she said.

"It isn't until tonight," I pointed out.

"Yes, but it's important to think about these things in advance. I couldn't possibly focus with the guests here."

"You wouldn't have to do that today if you hadn't left it until the last minute," I said. "You've had all week to decide what to wear."

"I don't know why you assume I know the day of the week, Rory," she said.

I gave an eye-roll. "Is Laney up?"

"Nope," she said. "Dead to the world, if you'll excuse the pun. How's Betsy getting on?"

"She's fine," I said. "Well, she's lecturing the patrons about how to write a mystery, but that's kind of harmless, right?"

"Of course she is," said Aunt Candace. "She can't help herself."

"Has she been publishing for long, then?" I asked.

"She's actually a new success in the mystery genre," said Aunt Candace. "She used to write literary fiction and thought writing mysteries was beneath her. Then her sales dried up, so she created a pen name and pretends she never belittled the rest of us for writing commercial fiction."

"Oh," I said. "Yeah, that doesn't surprise me, given what she said to me earlier. She implied you based the events in your books on the library."

"She's welcome to think whatever she likes," said Aunt Candace. "And I'll conveniently forget that she borrowed the plot in her first book from one of mine. What's Sylvester doing over there?"

I followed her gaze and spotted the tawny owl perching on top of a bookshelf near the Reading Corner.

"Listening to Betsy's lecture, apparently." Estelle walked over to join us.

"More like sleeping through it." Aunt Candace scoffed.

"He's already rearranged the guests' rooms twice today. Might make things more entertaining for them."

I suppressed a groan. "This is what we should have discussed before we nominated the library to host the event."

Like Cass, Sylvester didn't like sharing his space, and he was already annoyed at the idea of Laney staying in the library full-time. It'd taken him long enough to accept that *I'd* be staying here for the long-term, and for all we knew, having a bunch of strangers staying overnight might be enough to push him over the edge. He might appear to be nothing more than a familiar, but the owl had his own branch of powerful magic, even if most people didn't know the extent of it.

"I'll ask him to give it a rest," said Estelle. "Aunt Candace, can you watch the desk and wait for the guests? I expect more of them will start arriving soon, and my mum's busy tidying the guest rooms to get rid of Sylvester's meddling. He left a dead rat in one of them."

Aunt Candace tutted. "I suppose I can spare a few minutes."

"And Cass?" I asked. "I take it she isn't going to come down to help us out?"

"Is a broom made of sticks?" Aunt Candace guffawed at her own comment.

"I'll drop in and remind her we'd appreciate her help." Estelle made for the Reading Corner. "You two watch the desk, okay?"

"Don't even think about wandering off." I snagged Aunt Candace's sleeve as she made to turn away. "You're the one who volunteered us for this, in case you've forgotten."

Aunt Candace tugged herself free with a grumble, and then the door opened and a girl of around seventeen entered the library. She wore her brown hair in a high ponytail and had dressed in what looked like a school uniform, but not the uniform of Ivory Beach's local witch academy.

"Hey!" she said. "I'm here for the event."

"You're a nominee?" She looked like she was supposed to be at school, not here in the library, but the event didn't have an age limit on it.

"No, but I'm a huge fan of all the nominees," said the girl. "I'm Beverly. Are you Zora Martine?"

"I think you want my Aunt Candace." I pointed over my shoulder, spotting her slinking away towards the bookshelves. "She's just there."

"No *way.*" Beverly zipped to her side with almost vampire-level speed. Aunt Candace's brows shot into the air and she took a hasty step back as Beverly attempted to wrap her arms around her in a hug.

"I'm your biggest fan," Beverly gushed. "You're my idol. I have fifteen copies of each of your books."

I stifled a laugh at Aunt Candace's expression, a mixture of flattery and abject horror. "That's nice. Do you want to go and wait with the others? They're in the Reading Corner."

She looked so uncomfortable that I almost felt sorry for her. Despite her general self-confidence, she was surprisingly bad at taking compliments for her work and preferred to stay out of the limelight. While this might not be the first time she'd dealt with an overzealous fan, her commitment to secrecy meant most of her pen names never saw the light of day.

"Betsy Blake is in the Reading Corner," I told her. "You can probably hear her talking to the other patrons."

"Oh my *god*, I *love* her books," Beverly squealed. "I've always wanted to meet her."

And with that, she zoomed over to the Reading Corner like a human whirlwind. The instant she was gone, Aunt Candace vanished behind the bookshelves so efficiently that she might have given a vampire a run for their money herself.

"Relax," I told her. "I think she's after Betsy's autograph now. Come and help me out here."

As the door opened again, Aunt Candace shuffled back into view. This time, a witch wearing iron-grey robes sailed into the library.

"That's Winona Clair," she said out of the corner of her mouth. "She's the chair of the award committee."

"Welcome," I said to the witch when she approached the desk. "We're glad to have you here. Some of the guests have already arrived."

"Estelle!" Aunt Candace bellowed in the direction of the stairs. Then she turned back to the newcomer. "My niece is the social events coordinator here in the library. She'll be here in a second."

"Good," said Winona Clair, her gaze roving over the library. "Is this the venue for the ceremony?"

"Yes, but we'll move the shelves out of the way after the library closes for the night," I explained. "Oh, there's Estelle."

As my cousin walked into view, Winona hurried over to her to discuss the logistics of the night's event. Aunt Adelaide, meanwhile, was busy conjuring up an extra staircase near the Reading Corner which would enable the contenders to get to their guest rooms without venturing into our own living quarters. That left me to handle the front desk along with a reluctant Aunt Candace.

The noise from the back grew progressively louder as more guests joined the attending authors. I lost count of the number of people who tried to ambush Aunt Candace or asked me what it felt like to be the 'lost cousin'. One of them even tried to get me to sign her copy of the book based on my dad's life story, which I declined on the grounds that I'd had nothing to do with Aunt Candace's alter ego. The witch, who had dyed pink hair and matching nails, walked away in disappointment.

"That was Tiffany Wren," said Aunt Candace with her lips pursed. "She and I once wrote a book together, a few years back."

"Who's that?" I pointed out a witch wearing a midnight blue robe who'd brought a whole crate of copies of her own book along with her. She was also doused in perfume so strong that it stuck in my throat and made me cough long after she walked out of range.

"That," said Aunt Candace, "is Haylee Grace. Allegedly, she only ended up on the ballot because she bribed her family into voting for her. Or so the rumours say, anyway. She likes to attach herself to successful people in the hopes that it'll rub off on her."

"What's with the perfume?" I coughed again.

"Probably an attempt to cover up her other deficiencies." Aunt Candace glanced over to the Reading Corner. "Oh, Betsy's still lecturing everyone. I think she's advertising her marketing course."

Several of the patrons had come to complain about her

by now, but Betsy showed no signs of slowing down, and because she stood in such a prominent location, it was nearly impossible for the patrons to avoid her entirely.

"Can't you do something to stop her?" I said to Aunt Candace. "It's our library, after all."

"If she wants to blather away to anyone who wants to listen to her, she's welcome to," said Aunt Candace. "She's not going to win the prize, so she might as well have something to occupy her attention."

"Not sure the others will agree." Beverly was causing just as much trouble herself. She kept hassling people to give her their autograph, including those of us who weren't actually part of the event. Eventually, Estelle put her in charge of handing leaflets to the townspeople and convincing them to attend the award ceremony this evening.

Around noon, Xavier showed up in the library with a bag of food from Zee's bakery. The blond Reaper remained a total contrast to his fearsome boss, though his dark clothing and the scythe strapped to his back hinted at his real profession.

"Thought you needed sustenance," he said.

"You were right." I dug into the bag and pulled out a muffin. "Have you asked your boss whether you'll be allowed to come to the award ceremony this evening?"

The last time he'd been invited to a similar event at the library, the two of us had danced together for the first time. It had been a magical experience right up until his boss had shown up and utterly wrecked the mood. Incidentally, that'd been the moment I'd realised that trying to date the Grim Reaper's apprentice was a risky venture, yet we'd still made it work. His own job wasn't quite as busy as mine—which I was glad of, considering it involved escorting departed souls to the afterlife—but we both had little free time on our hands. I wouldn't have minded him attending the ceremony to keep me company. What with all the preparation for the event, we hadn't had a proper date in almost a week.

"I tried," he said. "He claims it'll distract me from my duties. Besides, are you sure you want to give Aunt Candace's friends any more incentive to put the two of us into their books?"

"Fair point." Being the 'lost cousin' was weird enough without everyone figuring out that I was in a relationship with the town's apprentice Reaper. "Someone's already tried to get my autograph just because Aunt Candace dedicated a book to me."

"Wow," said Xavier. "You're famous."

"I hope not," I said. "I prefer a quiet life. It's one of the few things Aunt Candace and I agree on."

We chatted for a while, until more people showed up and my lunch break came to an end. When Xavier left the library, I spotted Laney hovering near the opening of the corridor leading to our family's living quarters.

Leaving Estelle at the front desk, I went to talk to her. "You okay?"

"Sure," she said. "I thought I'd come and check out the action."

"Not much happening yet," I said. "It's not too noisy for you?"

"My room's far enough away that I can't hear everyone's thoughts." She glanced at the Reading Corner. "Okay, I can hear that woman going on about marketing, but I don't need to read her mind to do that."

"That's Betsy Blake," I said. "Might not be her real name, though. I think everyone in here is using aliases."

"Like spies," she said. "Maybe I should have come up with one, too."

Laughter came from behind me. I rotated on my heel, seeing a group of giggling students who were surreptitiously changing the colours of their teacher's hat when she wasn't looking.

"Hey." I walked over to them. "No magic in the library unless you're practising spells for class. That clear?"

The students ran off, still snickering, while I raised my eyebrows after them.

"Some things don't change, even in the magical world, huh," said Laney, with a grin.

"You bet." I walked back to her side. "Sure you're okay? I can move you to a different room tonight if it bothers you to be around so many other people."

"Nah, I don't sleep at night anyway," she said. "I'll nap through the ceremony instead."

The atmosphere had calmed a little by the evening, after the patrons had left and only the nominees for the award remained. In the hour between the library's closure for the night and the award ceremony, we took it in turns to run off to the living quarters and change into our best clothes, while Sylvester and Jet watched over the guests to make sure nobody ended up falling into the vampire's basement or getting lost in the stacks.

When my turn came, I ran back to my room to take a quick shower and then changed into a blue dress which had once been Cass's before she'd let me keep it in a surprising act of kindness which was probably never to be repeated again. I didn't have time to do anything fancy with my hair, but a wave of my wand dried it off, styling it into loose curls. Sending a silent thanks to Estelle for teaching me that spell, I went downstairs.

There, I found the lower floor of the library had transformed. Floating lanterns hovered around an open space where the shelves had folded back against the walls, leaving a circle of seats surrounding a wooden stage where Winona Clair stood under a spotlight. She waited for the others to fill in the seats, which Estelle had conjured up from the town hall with permission.

Within a few minutes, the guests began to file into the library, supervised by Aunt Adelaide, and made their way to the chairs circling the stage. I found a seat next to Estelle, who wore a nice deep-green dress with striking silver jewellery. I could see Sylvester perched on a shelf nearby, his owl-eyes barely blinking as he surveyed everyone in the audience. The contenders occupied the front row, including Aunt Candace, who wore her dazzling mirror-covered dress which made it difficult to look directly at her. No doubt that was her intention.

On the stage, Winona conjured up a sheet of paper and leaned over the microphone. Everyone quietened, ready to listen to her.

"It's my pleasure to welcome you all to this event, and I would like to offer my congratulations to everyone nominated for the Merry Mysteries award." She conjured up a huge glittering silver trophy, which floated in the air behind her. "This trophy is the grand prize, along with a substantial cash payment, and one lucky winner will claim both."

The trophy hovered in a halo of silvery light, and a series of fluttering blue birds flew out of it, eliciting gasps from the crowd. Tension gripped the entire room as Winona lifted the sheet of paper to read out the name of the winner.

"The winner of this prize," she said, "is Tiffany Wren."

Several people gasped. Tiffany herself looked like she might faint, while Aunt Candace shifted in her seat, the mirrors on her dress reflecting the gleaming trophy. The guests began to clap politely, which turned into loud applause as Tiffany rose to her feet. At some point she'd changed into a sequinned pink dress which matched her hair and nails.

In the front row, Betsy Blake went bright red. "How dare she? I was long overdue that prize. I have been waiting fifteen *years* for this!"

"Then you'll just have to wait a little longer." Tiffany sauntered up to the stage, where Winona handed over the trophy. Then she took the microphone and launched into an acceptance speech. It couldn't be clearer that Tiffany hadn't been prepared to win the prize, because her speech consisted of a twenty-minute ramble about her beloved dog, Mr Wrinkles. Nobody quite knew what to make of that, and her speech didn't come to an end until Winona cleared her throat and said, "That will be all, Tiffany. Congratulations."

"Thank you." She beamed. "I will have to call someone to take the trophy home for me... I can't possibly fly with it on a broomstick."

While she stepped aside, Winona prepared to read from her piece of paper again.

"The runners-up," said Winona, "will each get a small cash prize of their own. The two runners-up are Haylee Grace and Alana Flower."

The two runners-up ascended to the stage to receive their prizes. Haylee skipped up to the stage in the same midnight blue number she'd arrived in. Alana Flower, meanwhile, was a skinny witch with a tangle of dark hair whose wrinkled clothes looked as though she'd slept in them. She'd been one of the last to show up, and I wondered if she'd had a lie-in after staying up late working on her book and hurried straight here without bothering to change. If the ceremony hadn't been in the library, Aunt Candace might have ended up doing the exact same.

Betsy half rose to her feet, then slumped back into her seat. "This is unfair. *Unfair.* I deserve to be on that list."

"Betsy, please control yourself," said Winona. "If you have a problem, then feel free to talk to me after the ceremony is over."

Betsy gave a jerky nod, her shock as tangible as if someone had upended a vat of icy water on her head. "Yes, I'll do that. We'll discuss this terrible oversight later, mark my words."

"Honestly," Aunt Candace muttered audibly.

The rest of us clapped politely until the winners departed the stage. Then we rose to our feet at Winona's command. Aunt Adelaide waved her wand, causing the chairs to vanish and a couple of buffet tables to appear at one side of the library, while the stage itself turned into a dance floor.

Loud music followed, drifting from somewhere above our heads, and in no time at all, everyone was either dancing or raiding the buffet table. Everyone except for Betsy, that is, who was still shouting that her loss was a complete outrage at anyone who within earshot. Meaning

Beverly, who'd taken a break from scrounging for autographs to listen to Betsy's woes.

I wasn't a huge fan of big events where I didn't know many people, and I found myself wishing Xavier had been able to come. Admittedly, there was quite enough drama present in the library without adding the Grim Reaper on top of the contenders' gripes with one another, but Laney had also opted to sit this one out. I didn't blame her for it, but with Estelle in full hostess mode, I couldn't hang out with her either.

Instead, I looked for the one other person avoiding the crowds and found Aunt Candace hovering near the buffet cart. I'd expected her to be among the people complaining about not getting the prize, but she'd held up surprisingly well.

"At least I didn't have to make a speech," she said. "Terrible things, speeches. I'm glad Tiffany remembered to thank me at the end of hers."

"I thought you didn't like Tiffany," I said. "Are you okay with her winning the prize?"

"Better her than Betsy," she replied. "Fifteen years indeed. She only started writing two years ago. Or sooner. She's a pathological liar."

At that moment, Betsy burst into loud sobs in the middle of lamenting that there'd been a mistake. Aunt Candace broke out in a brilliant smile as though Christmas had come early, though she thankfully refrained from making any comments within earshot of her.

After imbibing copious amounts of wine, a few of the other guests ended up in the same state. Aunt Adelaide had to break up several fierce arguments, while Sylvester had long since vanished. Probably for the best, because he might have decided to deal with the problem by throwing Betsy into the vampire's basement or locking her in an upstairs corridor.

Admittedly, whenever I set eyes on Estelle, she looked like she wouldn't mind doing the same. Beverly, who I was pretty sure wasn't even old enough to drink, had passed out in the Reading Corner, so Betsy had spent the past hour wandering around the dance floor, looking for someone else to complain to.

"I should have got that prize," she hiccoughed, her face blotchy and her cheeks streaked with tears.

"Keep telling yourself that," said Tiffany from the other side of the dance floor. "Everyone knows you'll be weaselling your way into a different genre in a year's time and pretending you'd always been there."

Betsy pulled out her wand. *Uh-oh.* I looked around for the host, but Winona was engaged in a whispered conversation with Haylee Grace in the corner. Both of them were unsteady on their feet, holding wine glasses in their hands, and neither seemed to have noticed the sparks literally flying from the end of Betsy's wand.

Luckily, Aunt Adelaide stepped in. "That's enough, both of you. Betsy, I think you've had quite enough to drink. No magic in the library—either of you."

Tiffany sniffed loudly, putting her own wand away. "I'll be going now."

As she tottered away, Betsy dropped her wand and then tripped over it. While she scrambled to retrieve it, Tiffany let out a shriek. "Someone spilled wine on my trophy!"

Beverly chose that moment to vomit spectacularly all

over the bean bag she was lying on, diverting everyone's attention.

"I think," said Aunt Candace from behind me, "I am going to bed."

I was inclined to agree.

3

I woke to the thundering of footsteps above my head and outside in the corridor. I'd gone to bed early, so I hadn't seen how the night had ended. I gathered it'd been a late one, but it was beyond me to figure out why everyone was making a racket at this hour of the morning.

The hammering footsteps quietened. Then the shouting started, most of it unintelligible.

"It's the Reaper!" someone howled.

Xavier? I leapt out of bed, suddenly wide awake. It was unusual for Xavier to show up without texting, let alone early in the morning. I ran out of the room and followed the sound of shouting to a new, slightly crooked staircase which led up to the corridor containing the guests' rooms. Estelle must have conjured it up on the spot so she could go and see what the ruckus was about.

When I reached the top of the stairs, my gaze fell on Xavier's tall blond figure standing halfway down the corridor. Several heads peered out of the doors of the guest rooms, while Estelle was nowhere to be seen. Too late, it hit me that the Reaper wasn't here to pay a social call. He must be working. Which meant... someone had died.

He caught sight of me. "Rory."

"Hey." I walked towards him, conscious that I wore nothing but a pair of thin pyjamas and that the guests were now staring at the pair of us, putting two and two together. "What're you doing here?"

Stupid question, really, but everyone else looked hungover or generally confused. Betsy was almost unrecognisable now she wasn't wearing her glamour spells, while Haylee's bleary expression implied that she was still drunk. Only Alana looked exactly the same as she had yesterday, wrinkled clothes and all, holding a pen and notebook in her hand as if she'd been interrupted in the middle of a writing session.

"Hey, what's that?" Betsy pointed to the scythe on Xavier's back.

"He's the Reaper!" said Haylee, her face chalk white. "I told you so."

"I'm Xavier," he said to the others. "The Reaper's apprentice. I'm afraid it's bad news. Winona Clair is dead."

"You reaped her soul?" Tiffany said in a hushed voice. She looked as rough as the others did, with huge bags under her eyes and her pink lipstick smeared over her face as though she'd fallen asleep wearing it.

"That's my job, yes," said the Reaper. "I'm sorry for your loss."

Aunt Adelaide climbed up the stairs behind me, wearing a silky pink dressing gown. "What—oh, Xavier. Please tell me you're here to visit Rory, and not…"

"Winona Clair is dead," Haylee interjected. "How'd she die?"

"Can we see the body?" asked Alana.

Oh, boy.

"No," said Aunt Adelaide, "you may not see the body. Nobody move. I'm going to call the police—"

"I'm on it," Estelle yelled from downstairs. "Go back into your rooms, get dressed, and then come down to the lobby. Nobody is to leave the library."

An outburst rippled throughout the guests.

"You can't force us to stay in here," Betsy protested.

"Not if there's a killer on the loose," added Haylee.

As their arguments continued, I slipped back downstairs to my room before anyone sneaked in while I'd left it unattended. The noise was giving me a headache and I wasn't even hungover, and besides, leaving my dad's journal lying around at a time like this did not strike me as a good idea.

After quickly dressing, I left my room, hearing Estelle talking to the police on the phone from behind her half-open bedroom door. The new staircase linking the corridor to the guests' rooms upstairs had disappeared, so I went down into the lobby and headed for the Reading Corner to help Aunt Adelaide herd the guests downstairs.

While the guests were assembling in the Reading Corner, Estelle came into view, her hair wild and her eyes puffy. "Edwin's on his way. Where's the—body?"

"Winona is still in her room," Aunt Adelaide told her. "I asked Xavier to stand guard outside the door and make sure nobody goes in there until the police arrive, since he's the only person here who can be trusted not to turn this into a research opportunity. Has Candace even woken up yet?"

"I doubt even she slept through all that noise," I said. "Where's Sylvester? And Cass?"

"I have no idea." Estelle yawned. "I'm pretty sure Cass slept upstairs on the third floor with the animals. She probably hasn't heard anything yet. We're keeping everyone in the lobby until the police arrive, which should be any minute now."

The guests themselves seemed more fascinated by the murder than anything else, and though Cass was notably absent, I was inclined to agree with Estelle that she'd hidden upstairs to get away from the noise and might not have noticed anything was wrong. It wouldn't be the first time. I knew better than to think anyone in my family was responsible for Winona's death, so her absence didn't bother me, but it'd be nice to have her assistance in keeping the guests in line.

Edwin soon arrived with his two troll guards in tow. The elf policeman looked even smaller than usual with two hulking troll bodyguards and a tall wizard accompanying him.

Aunt Candace chose that moment to enter the lobby. "Did someone die?"

"I knew you weren't really asleep," said Aunt Adelaide. "Candace, stay here and make sure nobody leaves the Reading Corner. Edwin, Winona's body is upstairs in her room."

She led the way to the stairs up to the guest rooms, while the two trolls positioned themselves near the guests in the Reading Corner. Aunt Candace simply watched, her pen and notebook floating at her side, while I waited for Xavier to come downstairs. While I didn't want to give the guests any ideas about hassling the Reaper, I needed a touch of sanity in my life.

Xavier came downstairs a moment after the police had gone up to Winona's room, and he walked over to join me.

"Hey," I whispered. "Sorry about all the attention. You might want to leave if you don't want to show up in a dozen books."

"Hazards of the job," he whispered back. "It's fine. I can stay and keep you company."

"You don't have to," I insisted. "Besides, don't you need to report to your boss?"

"That can wait," he said. "Why do these things always happen to your family?"

Good question. "Xavier, did Winona say anything to you before you removed her soul? About how she died, I mean?"

"No, she was as surprised as anyone," he said. "She died in her sleep and doesn't remember anything else."

"Guess we'll find out, then," I said.

Several minutes passed before Edwin and the wizard came back downstairs, levitating Winona's body between them. I stepped aside to avoid being mowed over as the wizard followed Aunt Adelaide's instructions to take the body into one of the classrooms at the side of the Reading Corner.

I walked over to Edwin. "How'd she die, do you know?"

"Poison," said the elf. "We've yet to identify the specific type of poison, but there's no doubt that's what killed her."

"Poison?" someone said from the Reading Corner, and the air exploded with noise, questions and exclamations.

"Quiet!" Aunt Adelaide said.

It wasn't until the trolls turned on them, cracking their knuckles threateningly, that the crowd finally piped down. The trolls were generally pretty harmless, but their sheer bulk crammed into police uniforms made them look terrifyingly intimidating to most people.

"How'd they poison her?" asked Haylee. "Did they sneak into her room?"

"Or did they poison the wine?" someone else said. "She drank a whole bottle of the stuff last night, I saw."

"If any of you has any accurate information, then tell Edwin," said the wizard who'd levitated the body downstairs. "I will be examining the body to determine the type of poison that was used."

"In the meantime," said Edwin, "I will speak to everyone who was present in the library last night."

"It wasn't just us," said a haggard-looking Betsy Blake. "Half the town attended and a lot more besides."

The impossibility of the task sank in when I took in the disbelieving faces of the contenders. How many people had come to town just for this event? The library was open to the public, too, so anyone from Ivory Beach itself might've been here at some point or other.

"The library is where we'll start, since this is where she died," said Edwin. "Stay here."

He and Aunt Adelaide herded the guests further back into the Reading Corner, assisted by Estelle. Xavier and I supervised, and when we returned to the front desk, I noticed that Cass had slipped down into the lobby. "There you are."

She grunted. "I'm not surprised this event of yours ended in disaster, before you ask."

"You know someone died, right?" I said.

"Of course," she muttered. "It was obvious those guests were a few twigs short of a broomstick from the very start. The moment the winner was announced, I knew one of them would try something like this."

"Murdering the person who gave out the prize seems a little pointless, though," I said. "Weren't the winners voted on by a committee? Not just Winona herself?"

She shrugged. "Yes, but we're talking about a group of volatile creatives. Anyone might have decided Winona was to blame. I don't really care who did it as long as they don't stick around here."

That was Cass for you—as blasé as usual. "You might be hoping for too much."

Xavier walked over to join us. "I should head back to report to my boss, in case he comes here to check up on me. I don't think the guests need to meet the Grim Reaper."

"Wise idea." I hugged him goodbye. "Text me if you're free. I have a feeling I'll be marooned here for the weekend."

Most of the guests were staying for the rest of the day at least or until tomorrow morning, but who knew how long it would take the police to identify the culprit? With a bunch of mystery authors potentially involved, they might have gone to any lengths to hide their trail.

Edwin walked over to Cass and me after Xavier had left the library. "Which of you wants to talk to me first?"

"We're suspects?" Cass raised an eyebrow. "Why not

just arrest everyone who was nominated for that stupid prize?"

"Then you'd be accusing Aunt Candace, too," I reminded her.

Edwin grimaced, probably remembering when Aunt Candace had spent the night in a jail cell and spent the whole time driving the police out of his mind. "Your aunt isn't on my list of major suspects, but I hoped you could give me some insight into who might have done this. I'm guessing you weren't at the party?"

"Definitely not," said Cass. "I didn't even watch the ceremony and I spent the night upstairs with my animals."

"She's right," I said. "I was at the party, but I got an early night and I didn't see anything odd happen with Winona or the others. I know Betsy Blake was angry about missing out on the prize…"

"Betsy Blake?" said Edwin. "Her name has come up multiple times."

"I don't personally know any of these people," I said, "but Betsy had the strongest reaction to not winning. I'm surprised she wasn't asked to leave after the number of times she kicked up a fuss at the party."

If I asked all the other guests who their main suspect was, Betsy Blake would be the obvious choice. Her reaction to missing out on the prize had been hostile from the start, and the last time I'd seen her, she'd been drunkenly sobbing at anyone who would listen that she'd been deliberately spurned. If I had to pick anyone to accuse of having snapped and murdered the host, it'd have been her.

"Did you see anyone near Winona's room before her death?" he asked.

"No, but I was asleep," I said. "The party went on all

night, more or less. Will you be able to identify the poison and how it was administered? I think that would help."

"More worrying is that this seems to have been premeditated," he said. "A poison couldn't have been brewed on the spot, which means the guest brought it with them."

My heart lurched. "I never thought of that."

Did that mean the killer had known they would lose from the start? Or did they have another reason for targeting Winona which had nothing to do with the contest?

"Why didn't we search everyone's bags on the door?" said Cass.

"Because it would have taken too long," I said. "Besides, it's not a fool-proof method. The killer might've gone outside the library and used a spell to conjure the poison up and then used magic to get rid of the empty container after poisoning her. With magic involved, it's hard to keep track."

"No, they can't have conjured up anything," said Cass. "Sylvester was watching the doors all night. It's supposed to be his job."

"People were still coming and going throughout the day," I reminded her. "I don't know where Sylvester is at the moment, but I doubt he'll be thrilled if you accuse him of not taking his position seriously."

"I agree with Rory," said Edwin. "Almost everyone who attended the party had magic at their disposal which makes it unlikely that they left any careless evidence lying around. We found nothing at the scene of the crime. My guards are doing a thorough search of all the guests' possessions, but my guess is that the person who did this was careful to cover it up."

"Convenient," said Cass. "Just arrest this Betsy Blake and be done with it."

His expression darkened. "I will talk to the others. Do come and find me if you learn anything else, won't you?"

"Whatever," said Cass. "I take it I can go back upstairs now?"

"Do as you like." Cass's temper would not help matters down here, and besides, she hadn't seen any more than I had. Less, if anything, since she hadn't been to the ceremony *or* the after-party.

As she departed, I went to find Aunt Adelaide near the Reading Corner. "Oh, hello, Rory."

"Aunt Adelaide," I said. "Would the library's magic be able to detect if any of the guests cast a spell in here? I was thinking that if the killer used a spell to get rid of the evidence, then maybe we can find the culprit that way."

She shook her head. "There were too many people here last night. Too much magic. We should have kept a closer eye on everyone from the start."

"Sylvester." I spotted the owl flying overhead. "You were watching the party last night. Did you see anyone leave the library who was supposed to be staying here?"

He flew to a halt on top of a bookshelf. "Why would I have taken note of which of your tedious guests was supposed to be where?"

"Cass told me you were watching the doors all night," I said. "I thought the person who did this might have used a spell to get rid of the evidence, but the library can be oversensitive to magic use. If they'd disposed of the evidence outside the library, you'd have seen them leave, right?"

He scoffed. "I was only watching the doors up until that pixie took over from me."

"Where is he?" I couldn't see the pixie anywhere, but he tended to turn himself invisible when nervous or overwhelmed. Besides, only Estelle could understand his language, and she was surrounded by a crowd of complaining guests at the moment.

Sylvester made a tutting noise. "I have no interest in how that absurd creature spends his time. A waste of space, that one."

"Don't you start." I pinched the bridge of my nose. "No picking fights. We have quite enough conflict in here already."

"Yes, we do." Aunt Adelaide made for the front desk. "I'll keep an eye on things here, Rory. You should check up on your friend."

I looked where she pointed and saw Laney hovering near the corridor to our family's living quarters. If she didn't know what'd happened, then someone needed to tell her the others might be staying here for much longer than the allotted time.

Bracing myself, I approached her. "I don't know if anyone told you, but Winona Clair was murdered last night."

"I heard." She looked past me at the Reading Corner where the guests had gathered. "Did one of them do it?"

"Probably." I dropped my voice. "Were you awake late last night? Do you know if anyone was out of their room when they shouldn't have been?"

"Honestly, I thought they had free run of the library

anyway," she said. "I was awake, but I didn't come out of my room. Didn't the party go on until five in the morning?"

"Probably," I said. "I was asleep. Had to cast a soundproof spell on my room, too, but now I'm starting to wish I'd stayed downstairs to supervise."

Not that anyone would have been able to keep track of all the action, if the guests had been roaming the place as though they lived here.

Laney tilted her head. "I could have a sniff around the crime scene using my vampire super-senses. Would that help?"

Good thinking.

"I'll ask Edwin," I said. "The police haven't found anything yet, and Edwin said there's a good chance the killer used magic to cover their traces."

"Yeah, that's what I figured," she said. "I wouldn't know how to identify the poison or anything, but I thought it'd be good practise."

"Yeah, it would." If the wizards' spells didn't reveal anything, then we had a potential backup plan on our side. Assuming I wanted to risk Laney drawing the attention of everyone in the library, that is. None of them knew we had a vampire living here—or two, technically, given the one sleeping in the basement. Since he hadn't woken up in the last few decades, we'd opted not to tell the guests he existed. Laney, on the other hand, was considerably more difficult to hide.

"All right." She rubbed her forehead. "I'm going somewhere quiet. It's too loud in here."

"You go and have a nap," I said to her. "Let me know if you need anything, okay?"

After she'd gone back upstairs, I went in search of the pixie, but I found no signs of him aside from the ever-present glitter that he dropped all over everything in sight. Estelle might be able to coax him out of hiding, so I headed up to the Reading Corner where she was attempting to stave off the guests' questions. Aunt Candace, meanwhile, was being no help whatsoever, sitting in a chair with her notebook and pen. Taking notes, I assumed.

"Will everyone be patient?" Estelle said in exasperated tones. "You'll get your turn to talk to Edwin. No, you can't go to the shop, Haylee."

Edwin came out of the classroom he'd picked out for the questioning and beckoned Estelle to talk to him, while I walked over before the guests waylaid me, too.

"I'm sending some people to talk to the guests from out of town who are staying at the inn," Edwin said. "They all count as suspects, too."

"I know," Estelle said. "How long is this going to take? Everyone keeps asking when they can leave."

Edwin shook his head. "I believe the best move is to have them stay in town, at least until we can narrow down the list of who might have done this."

"There aren't enough rooms for everyone at the hotel," said Estelle. "But we can't let them stay in the library. Not when one of them is a potential murderer."

"There's not enough room in the prison either," he said. "We don't have enough holding cells for every single person who attended the event. I'm going to carry on with the questioning. The rest of you can sort out your plan among yourselves."

And with that, he returned to the classroom and called in the next person for questioning.

I looked at Estelle. "Is he serious?"

"Cass is going to be furious," said Estelle.

"You're really thinking of letting everyone stay here?" I said.

"I don't think we have a choice," said Estelle. "They're all using aliases. The instant they leave town, they could vanish off the face of the earth and we'd never catch them."

"That's no reason to put everyone in here in danger." I turned towards the front desk, where Aunt Adelaide stood. "Guess we need to tell your mum."

Aunt Adelaide didn't seem surprised at the news when we told her. "I don't like it, but we can secure the library thoroughly so there's no chance of anyone committing another crime."

"Better hope someone confesses before tonight, then," I said. "Has anyone let anything slip so far?"

"Not according to Edwin," said Estelle. "They all have varying stories about where they were during the night's events, but I have a feeling it'll take a while to sort it all out."

"And that's assuming they remember accurately, considering how drunk everyone was," I added.

"I should have seen something like this coming," said Aunt Adelaide. "It's my fault."

"No, it's mine," said Estelle. "I'm the one who organised the party. I should have worked out how to make it easier to keep an eye on everyone."

"This is the library we're talking about," I said. "It's

impossible to watch everyone at the same time, even when they aren't drunkenly partying."

"Which is why we shouldn't have agreed to host the event here to begin with," said Aunt Adelaide. "I know Candace suggested it, but I'm the one who gave the go-ahead."

"You've held events here before, right?" I said. "You hardly expected a murder to happen. Besides, this has nothing to do with the library. If one of the other venues had been chosen, like the castle, then the murderer would have struck there instead. Knowing Aunt Candace, she'd probably have refused to leave until she found the answer."

"At least we're here to stop Aunt Candace from getting caught up in the mayhem alone, I suppose," said Estelle. "Not that she seems bothered."

"Looks more like she's using it as a research opportunity," I said, with an eye-roll. "She's not the only one, either."

I cast a glance over the Reading Corner and saw Betsy Blake standing in the centre of the gathering guests. She cleared her throat loudly, drawing the attention of everyone in the area.

"I would just like to state, for the record, that I had nothing to do with Winona's death."

Mutters passed among the guests. It couldn't be more obvious that most of them didn't believe her, but then again, I wasn't sure I did either. She hadn't acted innocent at all.

"I know I was upset yesterday," she went on, "but I wouldn't *kill* someone for not giving me a prize."

Another murmur of general disagreement travelled

through the surrounding guests, and her shoulders drooped.

"A likely story," Haylee Grace said flatly. "You're going to jail, and good riddance."

"If you ask me," said Betsy, "it was you who did it, Haylee. I saw you arguing with Winona last night. And you were one of the last to return to your room when the party was over."

"Enough!" Aunt Adelaide's tone was sharper than I'd ever heard from her. "No fighting among yourselves. Unless you'd like me to hand you over to Edwin, that is."

"I would prefer that not to happen either." Edwin peered out of the classroom. "I'll speak to all of you individually. Please try to be patient until then."

While he withdrew into the room again, Betsy Blake waylaid Aunt Adelaide. "I was telling the truth," she insisted. "I didn't kill her."

Aunt Adelaide gave her a pitying look. "I'm not the person you need to convince, Betsy."

"Look, if you must know, I decided to get an early night. Earlier than the rest of you, anyway," she said. "Winona was still down at the party at the time."

"Tell Edwin that, not me," said Aunt Adelaide. "There's nothing I can do about it."

Betsy Blake wilted on the spot. "I'm too hungover for this. It's not fair."

"So say we all," Estelle said. "Go on, sit down with the others. The quicker you cooperate, the quicker this will be over."

With a sniff, Betsy returned to join the other guests, all of whom gave her a wide berth. A moment later, Edwin's wizard assistant came out of the neighbouring classroom and went to exchange a few words with Aunt Adelaide.

"Estelle, Rory," Aunt Adelaide beckoned us both over. "Can you watch the front desk? I'm going to help Gregor here examine the body so we can figure out what type of poison was used."

"Isn't that more Aunt Candace's area of expertise than yours?" said Estelle.

"Yes, but she's still theoretically on the suspect list." Aunt Adelaide's mouth pinched in a frown. "I'll have to do the best I can."

Estelle heaved a sigh. "I'll go and put up a sign on the library door saying we're closed for the day, then."

I walked alongside her towards the front desk. "Is the pixie around?"

"Why?" she asked.

"Sylvester claimed he was supposed to be watching the door last night," I said. "I wondered if the killer went outside to get rid of the evidence. Maybe someone saw."

"Oh." Her brow crinkled. "Perhaps, but I doubt the killer would have been that obvious about it. Everyone here researches crimes for a living, remember?"

"No kidding." I cast my mind around in an attempt to figure out who could outsmart an expert aside from one of their own. "How are we supposed to make the place secure, though? I doubt some of them will take kindly to having to spend another night here."

"We could lock the place down," she said. "Stop anyone from using magic at all."

I raised a brow. "Is that even possible?"

"It's possible, but the library wouldn't like it a bit," she said.

"Bet the others won't either," I said. "Are you going to do that?"

"Not yet," she said. "They already handed their wands over to Edwin, so there's no danger of them hexing one another. There *is* a toned-down version of the spell which would stop anyone from using transportation magic to sneak out and run away, so we can use that one."

"Good idea," I said. "If someone is always watching the door, then nobody can leave without being caught by one of us."

"Exactly." She pulled out her Biblio-Witch Inventory. "Want to help me out?"

I hesitated. "This is a new spell, right?"

"Yes, but it'll work better if there are two of us."

I took out my notebook and pen, then pressed the point of it to the page. At Estelle's instruction, I wrote the word *bind*.

"All right," she said. "Ready?"

A shiver ran from my fingertips to the pen, and we both tapped the word *bind* at the same time. Magic flooded my hand, and light swirled around our heads, spreading through the air and dissipating around us.

"Did it work?" I asked.

"Try the travel spell."

I pulled out my Biblio-Witch Inventory and hit the word *travel*. A faint breeze rose up, but the library remained in place, and we hadn't moved an inch.

"Write the new spell into your Biblio-Witch Inventory," Estelle said. "Nicely done."

4

The questioning continued for the rest of the morning. Opening the library to the public was out of the question, so Estelle put a sign outside saying that the place was closed until the end of the weekend.

"They'll all be talking about it," Estelle said dismally. "This isn't even the first time someone has been murdered here, which makes the whole situation worse."

"But this time it's someone from outside town," I said. "And none of us are suspects."

"There is that." She exhaled in a sigh. "I can't believe I let this happen on my watch. I should have at least asked Sylvester to watch the guests' corridor, considering all those accusations of stealing ideas and manuscripts... not to mention the arguments over the prize."

"Don't start blaming yourself," I said. "Same with Aunt Adelaide. It's not your fault."

"But the library is ours," she said. "We're responsible for it."

"You're not responsible for everything that happens in here," I said firmly. "Also, these are authors we're talking about. They're creative. Even if you did have a way to keep an eye on them, they might have found a way around it anyway. It's what they do."

"Fair point," she said.

"Also, Laney volunteered to look at the crime scene and have a sniff around," I added. "I wanted to ask Edwin's permission, but I think it's better if I wait until his people are done searching the crime scene before we go in."

"Oh, good thinking," she said. "How is Laney, anyway? I never asked."

"Fine, but a little freaked out by the whole thing," I said. "She planned to avoid the main part of the library throughout the event, but if the guests are going to stick around, I don't know how she'll cope. She said the noise is bothering her quite a bit."

"Nothing we can do," said Estelle. "The police flat-out refuse to let everyone go home as long as they're all suspects, and there's nowhere else they can stay. Besides, maybe it's best to keep them in one place until someone confesses."

"I guess." If that was the case, I could say goodbye to getting a moment's peace with my dad's journal before the end of the weekend.

Leaving the sign affixed to the door, Estelle returned to the front desk, while I went back to the Reading Corner to ask Edwin about getting Laney's assistance in searching the scene of the crime. There, Betsy Blake had slumped into a bean bag as though she wished it would swallow her up. Aunt Candace sat opposite her, her pen floating in mid-air and scribbling on a notepad at her side.

I walked over to her. "Don't you think that's in poor taste?"

"I don't see anyone complaining," she said.

"That's because they're all scared of being arrested," I said. "I take it you're confident you aren't a suspect at all?"

"I already spoke to Edwin," she said. "I told him the truth: that I left the party early and retired to bed. I don't even sleep on the same floor as the rest of you, so it's easy enough to verify that I was nowhere near the crime scene. Besides, I liked Winona. She was a character."

I arched a brow. "Did you put her in one of your books?"

"Maybe once." She tutted. "Poison. It's such an unimaginative method. If you ask me, it has Betsy's name written all over it."

"Are you sure?" I asked. "Don't get me wrong, it'd be a relief to put all this behind us, but there were a *lot* of people here in the library last night and the police still haven't found any evidence yet. As long as they don't have anything to go by, all we have is guesswork."

"The most obvious choice might not be the correct one," she said. "Yes, if I were writing this into a book, I'd use Betsy to distract from the real culprit."

"Exactly," I encouraged. If I could convince Aunt Candace to see this as a useful exercise, I might actually get her to help in a constructive manner rather than sitting around eagerly scribbling in a notebook while the rest of us did all the work. "Anyone else who might be hiding a secret?"

"We're authors," she said. "We all have twisted secrets. Or if we don't, we make them up."

That figured. "Would anyone have a reason to murder Winona, though? Something specific to her, and not necessarily connected to the contest?"

Aunt Candace pursed her lips. "I suppose... hmm. Winona was a known busybody in certain circles. She caused a fair bit of division when she was elected as the chair of the award committee. Tiffany never liked her."

"Really?" I said. "Tiffany won the prize, though."

"Oh, the vote-in system is anonymous, so it wasn't Winona who picked the winner, really." She tutted. "It's more of a popularity contest than anything else, which is one reason why Betsy never stood a chance of winning. She's too recent to the genre, and she's burned too many bridges with her peers."

At that moment, Haylee emerged from the questioning room with a self-satisfied look on her face. "That's that taken care of. Winona clearly made an enemy at the wrong time, but it had nothing to do with me. I'm more than ready to get out of this place and go home."

"You can't go home until Edwin dismisses all of you," I reminded her, since nobody else seemed inclined to say anything.

"Where's Alana gone, then?" asked Hayley.

"Who's Alana?" I said. "Oh—the other runner-up. Is she with Edwin?"

"No," said Aunt Candace, looking away from her notebook. "She seems to have vanished."

"She can't have left." I gave the area a scan, remembering the skinny witch who'd shown up at the award ceremony dressed as though she'd walked out of a long writing session. "I thought Sylvester was supposed to be watching everyone."

"Don't look at me," said Aunt Candace.

So much for keeping everyone in one place.

"I'll check with Estelle," I said. "Maybe she got lost somewhere."

Trying to suppress my annoyance, I went back to the front desk, where Estelle sat with her head resting on her folded arms. Hearing my approach, she looked up and rubbed her tired eyes.

"Hey," I said. "Have you seen Alana Flower?"

"No, why?" she said. "Which one was she?"

"The other runner-up," I said. "She was dressed like Aunt Candace is when she comes out of her research cave, but it sounds like she's disappeared somewhere in here. Did you see anyone leaving?"

"No." She groaned. "Can Sylvester search for her?"

"I'd ask him if I knew where he was." I could see Jet flitting around the shelves near the front desk, but the owl was presumably watching the Reading Corner from afar. Or maybe hiding with Cass. "I'll search the ground floor."

Since all the classroom doors downstairs were shut and the place was pretty tidy by the library's standards, it didn't take long for me to determine that Alana wasn't anywhere within sight.

"No luck?" Aunt Candace called out to me when I walked past her chair on my way back through the Reading Corner. "Sure she hasn't fallen into the vampire's basement?"

"I'd rather not open it to check right now."

She bared her teeth in a grin. "Wish I'd locked Betsy Blake in there."

"Maybe she went back to her room," I said, ignoring her vindictive chuckling. "I'll check."

I headed for the staircase leading up to the guests' quarters. Or rather, where the stairs had once been, because now the guests' corridor ended abruptly with the floorboards cutting off in mid-air. That was new.

"Help!" said a voice from the upper corridor.

"Who's up there?" I called out, suspecting I already knew the answer.

"It's Alana Flower," she called back. "I can't get down."

"Hang on," I said. "I can help you out."

I pulled out my wand and waved it, moving an armchair from the Reading Corner and positioning it in the spot where the stairs had once been.

Alana peered over the edge. "You expect me to jump?"

"Unless you want me to levitate you down, this is the best I've got," I said.

"The police confiscated all our wands," she said in petulant tones. "Can't you put the stairs back? You do live here, don't you?"

"Yes, I do," I said, growing annoyed. "I expect the person who moved the stairs was trying to stop people from wandering out of bounds without permission. Didn't my aunt and Edwin tell you not to run off?"

"I didn't know I wasn't allowed up here," she protested. "Can you levitate me down? Please?"

"All right." I reached into my pocket and pulled out my Biblio-Witch Inventory, then hit the word *fly*.

At once, Alana sailed off the edge of the upstairs corridor, landing awkwardly on the armchair beneath. I released a relieved breath, glad that I hadn't dropped her by accident.

"Why were you upstairs, anyway?" I asked.

"I had to get my notebook," she said. "My spare one, I mean. I need to take more notes for my next book. Besides, I didn't want to leave it up there in case someone sneaked into my room to read it. I wouldn't put it past certain people."

Uh-huh. She might be telling the truth, but my paranoia was hard to shake with nobody acting innocent in the slightest. It didn't help that half the guests were experts on researching murder and the police had explicitly told them not to wander out of bounds.

"Sure you weren't trying to get to the crime scene?" I asked.

"I didn't know Winona that well," she said, though the faint flush on her face suggested I'd guessed right. "Besides, all I want is to go home. I have a conference on Monday, and I can't stay here indefinitely."

"Has Edwin questioned you yet?"

"Not yet, no," she said. "I assumed he was gradually working his way through his list, starting with the most likely suspects."

"He is, but it doesn't help when people run off to do their own thing," I said. "It's lucky it was just the stairs that vanished."

"This place is mad," she muttered to herself. "Stairs shouldn't disappear. What did Candace do to this place?"

Don't blame her, blame my grandmother. Not only was Grandma the library's creator, she'd never left a map behind after her death. Rather like my dad and the journal situation, except I'd at least found the translation for that. As a result of Grandma's antics, even my family had yet to unearth all the library's secrets, and I sometimes forgot how odd the library was even by the magical world's standards until I saw how other people from outside of the town reacted to it.

When I returned to the Reading Corner, Edwin was between questionings, so I went to waylay him before he disappeared into the classroom again.

"Rory," he said. "What is it? I'm busy."

"I have a quick question," I said. "Would Laney be able to help search the crime scene? She's a vampire, so perhaps she can sniff out something that hasn't been picked up by your wizards or other staff."

"I suppose it couldn't hurt at this stage," he said. "I'll check with the others."

He went to speak to the two trolls standing on either side of the gathering guests, and then called on the wizard who'd gone into the neighbouring classroom with Aunt Adelaide to examine Winona's body.

After they exchanged a few words, the wizard approached me. "Your vampire friend has volunteered to look at the crime scene, has she?"

"If it's okay," I said. "She has a better sense of smell than the rest of us. She might be able to pick up on a clue about the poison, or even get a sense of who else might have been in the room."

"All right," he said. "I can't say I've ever had a vampire volunteer to help us out at a crime scene before."

"I guess not," I said. "Evangeline is only bothered when it's her own people involved."

I doubted she cared in the slightest that someone had died here in the library. Though I did expect her to come back and try to recruit Laney at some point, I had little doubt that she'd wait until the guests had gone and we'd let our guard down. She wouldn't want to get involved in this.

"Precisely," said Edwin. "But please don't spread word among the others."

I glanced over my shoulder to confirm nobody was listening in. "I don't want all the guests to know we have a vampire in the library. I'll be quiet, don't worry."

I went looking for Laney, only to find she'd disappeared again. After failing to find her in the living quarters, I recalled her ongoing quest to get into the Vampire Section on the first floor. This didn't seem a good time for her to go wandering off, though it was admittedly quieter up there than down among the guests. Maybe she'd gone to check if the door had returned to its proper place while she waited for permission to go to the crime scene.

I walked up to the first floor and heard a scuffling noise from somewhere behind the shelves. Looked like my hunch was right. I circled the shelves and found Laney beside the door to the Vampire Section, which was half open in front of her.

"Hey, Laney," I called to her. "What're you doing?"

She spun on her heel, guilt flickering across her features. "Uh, Rory, there's a problem."

"What?" I said warily.

"I may have left the door open a crack..."

My heart swooped. "And?"

"And the book wraith got out."

5

I looked at Laney for a moment. "You're joking."

"Do I look like I'm joking?" She pushed the door firmly shut. "I think it slithered under a bookshelf somewhere around here, but I can't hear it. Does that mean it's left the area?"

"No, but it's very stealthy," I said. "Maybe too quiet even for vampire hearing."

"Figures." She sprang over to the nearest shelf and peered underneath. "It happened so fast. That thing moves quicker than a vampire does."

"I can help you look, but I might need to conjure up a torch."

In this particular section of the library, shadows filled almost every available space between the shelves, making it impossible to pinpoint a creature which could crawl under any surface and liked feeding on ancient languages. Of all the things to escape, it had to be the most impossible to find. Though at least it wasn't Cass's manticore.

I cast a light charm and stuck my wand underneath the

shelf to see if I could surprise it, but the creature tended to hide away from light and there was no shortage of hiding places. After searching under every shelf in the vicinity, I caught sight of Sylvester perched on the balcony and went over to talk to him.

"Sylvester, I need your help," I said.

"With what?" he said. "I'm in charge of late fees, not herding your obnoxious visitors around."

"That's not what I wanted to ask," I said. "Laney accidentally left the door to the Vampire Section open and the book wraith got out. Have you seen any strange shadows lately?"

Sylvester hooted with laughter, to no surprise. "Excellent. That'll inject some excitement into our lives."

"Isn't the murder investigation enough on its own?" I said. "We don't need everyone terrorised by a creepy shadowy monster as well."

"Maybe it'll convince the culprit to confess faster," he said.

"The wraith won't actually do anything to the guests, will it?" I said warily. "I thought it was harmless."

"If left to its own devices, it is," he said. "If one of those guests provokes it, though?"

"Are you serious?" I folded my arms. "Sylvester, I'll give you freedom to attack all the balloons you like when the guests are gone if you help me out here."

"I don't accept bribery," he said. "I'd rather they were gone as soon as possible."

"Look, it'll derail Edwin's questioning if he's interrupted by a book wraith, won't it?" I said. "Can't you at least keep an eye out for where it might be hiding? You can fly. It's not that hard to watch for mysterious shadows."

"I can't see underneath the shelves, you lampshade," he said. "I'm not *that* talented."

"Neither can I, and I can't fly, either," I pointed out. "Is the book wraith likely to have left this floor? If not, then it'd be simple to spot it on the stairs. You don't even have to move. Just watch for movement and report back to me."

"I suppose." Sylvester gave a prolonged exaggerated sigh. "I will endeavour to watch for your escaped monster, then."

While the owl perched on top of a nearby shelf, I resumed my search. Considering the bookshelves sometimes moved around, searching underneath them seemed a tad redundant, but the wraith was most likely to be as close to the books as possible.

Hearing a yell, I wriggled out from under the shelf and hit my forehead on the edge. Stifling a yelp of pain, I rose to my feet and looked around for the source of the noise. Two voices drifted up from below, steadily growing in volume.

Oh, no. That was Aunt Candace shouting.

"Be right back!" I called over my shoulder to Laney as I ran for the stairs.

I descended as fast as I could without slipping on a trick stair, following the sound of Aunt Candace's voice. I didn't have to look far. Aunt Candace stood in the entryway to our family's living quarters, wearing an incandescent expression on her face. Opposite her stood Tiffany Wren, winner of yesterday's prize and my aunt's ex-cowriter.

"What's going on?" I asked breathlessly.

"She was peeking at my manuscript," said Aunt Candace. "Don't deny it."

"I wasn't," Tiffany protested. "I didn't know I wasn't allowed to walk around."

"This whole area is off-limits," said Aunt Candace. "Besides, Edwin told you to stay put."

"I can't stand to be around those people," she said. "They're all being obnoxious. You have a whole library here, why not use it?"

"Because you're untrustworthy," said Aunt Candace. "And you're murder suspects, too. We're not letting you roam around in the library without anyone watching you."

"We can't all have committed the murder," said Tiffany. "We can't all stay here indefinitely, either. It's absurd."

"It won't be indefinite if we find the culprit," I interjected. "Tiffany, I don't know what you were doing in there, but it's not a good time to be roaming around our family's private living quarters."

"I'm hardly the only one," said Tiffany. "I saw Haylee hanging around here earlier."

Aunt Candace's eyes narrowed. "*She* wants to look at my manuscript, I don't doubt, but that doesn't get you off the hook."

"I didn't know this area was out of bounds," said Tiffany. "I don't need to sneak a look at your manuscript, either."

"Anyone would think you were incapable of thinking of any new ideas of your own," said Aunt Candace.

"Keep telling yourself that. I'm the one who won the

prize, remember?" Tiffany turned her back and walked away, back towards the Reading Corner.

I rubbed my throbbing forehead. "Do you think she was really trying to get her hands on your manuscript? Because she must know how suspicious it looks when she wanders off while the police are doing their questioning."

"Yes," she said. "Things have been strained whenever we've met in person since we stopped working together, but I don't see her as a potential murderer. Besides, I know her methods. I worked with her on a mystery series, remember?"

Hmm.

"Alana Flower claimed to be looking for something in her room, too," I added. "I found her stuck on the upper floor. The stairs moved and left her with no way down."

"I know they did. I'm the one who moved them."

I blinked. "Did you know Alana was stuck up there when you did it?"

"Of course not," she said. "Why would I?"

"I don't know." I rubbed my forehead again, suspecting a bruise was forming from where I'd hit it on the shelf earlier. That probably wasn't helping me think any clearer, either. "She claimed to be looking for her spare notebook, but I think she might have wanted a peek at the crime scene instead."

Aunt Candace scowled. "That or she wanted to sneak out."

"She can't," I said. "Estelle and I put a spell on the whole library preventing anyone from using magic to get out."

"Good idea." She sounded pleased. "That'll teach them."

"Did Alana know her well?" I asked. "Winona, I mean?"

"Not that I'm aware of," she said. "It's got to be Betsy who did it. No evidence necessary."

"Edwin also gave me permission to take Laney to have a sniff around the crime scene," I added. "I can't do that if we can't get up to Winona's room, though. Can you put the stairs back where they belong?"

"Well, all right," she said. "Where is your friend, anyway?"

"Well, there's another issue," I said. "A book wraith is on the loose from the Vampire Section."

"What do you expect me to do about that?" she said. "Did your friend let it out, by any chance?"

"It was an accident," I clarified. "If you see it down here, can you let me know? We need to check the crime scene, but if that wraith goes near the guests, it'll send everyone into a panic again."

"That'd be entertaining, though." As I gave her a warning look, she said, "Fine, I'll keep an eye out. And I'll put the stairs back, too."

"Thanks." Leaving Aunt Candace behind, I hurried back upstairs to the first floor to find Laney.

Sylvester looked down at me from his perch on the bookshelf. "Dealt with your aunt, have you?"

"For now," I said. "Where is Laney?"

"She went upstairs," he said. "The third floor, I believe."

"Why would she…?" I trailed off. Cass was up there, so Laney must have gone to ask for her help. As if *that* wouldn't end badly.

"I'd leave her to it," said the owl. "If she wants to get attacked by a manticore, it's on her."

"Not funny, Sylvester." Cass usually kept her pets securely locked up, but then again, she was probably the person here who was most qualified to deal with the book wraith. Not necessarily without causing a scene, though. I hadn't forgotten the time a kelpie had got loose in here. Not to mention the boggart… and the manticore.

I ran up to the third floor and found Laney standing outside the wooden door leading to Cass's favoured part of the library.

"Is your cousin Cass somewhere in there?" she asked. "I can't get the door open and she isn't answering."

"Believe me, it's probably better off if she doesn't open the door," I said, "in case something worse than the wraith gets out. Hang on, I'll talk to her."

I approached the wooden door, hearing scuffling noises from the corridor behind it, and I rapped on the surface with my knuckles. No answer, so I knocked again. "Cass, I know you're in there."

"What?" came the muffled reply.

"We need your help," I said to her. "Or to be more precise, there's a magical creature which needs your help."

This time, the door cracked open and Cass's face appeared in the gap. "What is going on this time?"

"The book wraith escaped," I said. "And we don't know where it went."

"Oh, for the love of…" She cut off in a growl of annoyance. "Can't you find it yourself?"

"You're the expert." Like with Sylvester, it was best to use flattery to get through to Cass. "Also, Laney has permission to go and sniff around the crime scene to find the killer, but we can't do that and hunt for the wraith at the same time. We've looked all over the first floor."

Her eyes narrowed. "Oh, fine. I'll handle it."

"Thanks, Cass," I said gratefully. "Laney and I will

come and help out after we've finished with the crime scene."

"I doubt I'll need your help."

Let's hope not. Unable to believe she'd really said yes, I returned to Laney's side. "We have the all-clear to go to the crime scene, while Cass hunts down the wraith. With Sylvester's help, if necessary."

"You sure she'll follow through?" she said sceptically.

"I think she will," I said. "C'mon."

We went down to the lowest floor once again. As we reached the foot of the stairs, one of Edwin's trolls approached. "You said your friend wanted to search the crime scene?"

"Yes, she does," I said. "We had a bit of a distraction upstairs, but that's sorted now."

I hoped it was, anyway. I'd been right in saying Cass was the expert, so she ought to be able to track down the book wraith before it got anywhere near the guests.

In the meantime, Laney and I made our way to the far edge of the Reading Corner, where the stairs led up to the guests' rooms and the crime scene.

"Oh, good," I said, seeing the stairs were back in place. "Aunt Candace did put them back."

"She moved the stairs?" said Laney. "To stop people from getting at the crime scene, I take it?"

"And to stop them from getting at one another's unfinished manuscripts," I said, with an eye-roll. "Come on. Let's see what the killer left behind."

6

Laney and I climbed the stairs and walked down the corridor towards the room where Winona had been found dead. I let Laney overtake me, her graceful steps carrying her into the vacated guest room. Her feet made no impact on the carpet, which made me reluctant to follow after her in case I knocked something over with my clumsy human limbs. The room appeared undisturbed, though Winona's belongings had been removed, leaving nothing but the basic furniture which had already been in all the guest rooms.

"Sense anything?" I asked Laney.

"I can smell perfume," she said. "And... hmm. Troll."

"That'd be Edwin's guards," I said. "I guess you can smell everyone who's been here since the murder as well as beforehand."

"Yeah," she said. "You all have unique scents. Humans are different from elves, and trolls, and other magical creatures."

"I was hoping you might be able to smell the person who came in here and killed her," I said.

"So was I, but I can only smell the perfume," she said. "It's powerful enough that I can hardly even smell the trolls."

I walked in further. I could smell faint traces of a floral fragrance, too. "Haylee Grace was wearing that perfume."

But did that mean she'd committed the murder? Perhaps she'd been in the room for another reason. It wasn't like we could call up Winona's ghost and ask... I mean, technically we could, but I doubted I'd be able to get the rest of my family to agree to that idea. Besides, we had quite enough monsters in the library without adding a ghost on top of the book wraith currently roaming the first floor. And if Winona hadn't mentioned anything to Xavier which pointed to her killer when he was escorting her to the afterlife, then there was no reason to summon her ghost for a second questioning which wouldn't get us anywhere.

Laney walked around the bed once again, then shook her head. "Nothing else. I wouldn't know how to identify a particular kind of poison by scent, and besides, I imagine the police will figure that part out soon enough. Or your Aunt Adelaide will."

"I'll talk to Haylee and see if she'll admit why her perfume is all over the crime scene." Admittedly, that stuff was pungent enough that faint traces lingered in the corridor as well, but it was the only piece of evidence we had.

"Sure, why not," said Laney. "I think I should help your cousin find that book wraith in case she sets it loose on me as payback for invading her life."

"She won't," I said. "Not if I have anything to do with it, anyway. "

Laney shot me a sideways look. "She doesn't want me here. It's obvious."

"She didn't want *me* here for the first few weeks," I said. "Then I saved her life a couple of times. All you have to do is swoop in and save her neck from the book wraith and you'll be BFFs."

She cracked a grin. "Nah, I only have one best friend here."

I smiled back at the reminder that our friendship remained intact even after all the upheavals we'd faced recently. "Okay, let's move."

We returned to the Reading Corner to find that Betsy had started up another one of her lectures on her future marketing business to everyone within range. The others weren't even pretending to pay attention, while Beverly was scrounging for autographs from anyone who would listen to her.

Edwin's wizard assistant beckoned Laney and me into an alcove when he spotted us.

"Find anything in Winona's room?" he asked.

"I only smelled perfume," said Laney. "I didn't smell which type of poison was used or anything like that."

"No worries," he said. "I believe Adelaide is close to identifying the poison type which was used to kill the victim, but if there was nothing in her room to suggest the poison was given to her while she slept, there's a chance that they may've slipped it into her drink while she was downstairs. That's why it's vital that we get an accurate picture of where everyone was at the time."

"They poisoned her drink?" That meant the perfume

might mean nothing at all, if Winona had been poisoned before she'd gone to her room. "We didn't find anything else. Unless you want to have a sniff around here, Laney?"

She shook her head. "There are far too many people around for me to be able to tell whose scents came from last night."

"That's fine," I said, turning back to the wizard. "Can you pass on word to Edwin?"

"I will, when he's finished with the questioning," he responded.

We left Edwin's assistant and skirted the Reading Corner around the back route to avoid being accosted by any of the remaining guests. I didn't blame Laney for being overwhelmed. The library hadn't been so busy in a long time, and she wasn't usually in the thick of the action.

"Are you okay?" I asked Laney.

"Yeah, it's just the noise." She grimaced. "I can hear everyone's thoughts at the same time, and it sounds like rocks falling onto my head."

"You can hear..." Wait a moment. "I don't suppose there's a chance you heard who killed Winona?"

She rubbed her forehead. "Don't you think I'd have told you if I had? It's all a load of incoherent noise to me."

"How close would you need to be to read an individual person's thoughts?" I asked. "I mean, one person on their own, without anyone else around?"

"I don't know," she said. "Maybe a few feet away, but I'm not volunteering to join the police to help them with murder investigations, Rory."

I flushed. "I know. I'm not volunteering you either. I'm

just thinking about how this mess might drag on for days unless we find a shortcut somewhere."

But unless I found a way to get each potential suspect in the same room as Laney, one at a time, there wouldn't be a good method of getting the right information. Even then, it was possible that they'd had practise in hiding their thoughts from vampires. Besides, if word made it back to Evangeline that Laney was helping out in a police investigation, it might lead to her coming here to hassle Laney into joining up with her fellow vampires again.

"I know," Laney said. "I'll think about it, okay?"

"Sure," I said, feeling guilty for even bringing it up. "I suppose what we really need is an accurate picture of what happened last night, and to be honest, it'd be hard to get that even from reading everyone's minds."

"Yeah." She rubbed her eyes and yawned. "I think I'm going to take a power nap. Didn't get much sleep yesterday."

"Sure, you go and get some peace and quiet." I turned to the back of the library, debating whether to head over there and ask Haylee how her perfume had ended up all over Winona's room. I'd rather not ask her in front of an audience, though, and when I heard Alana telling some of the others about the disappearing staircase, I went to the front desk instead to avoid being dragged into that one.

Estelle arched a brow at me. "What's going on back there?"

"Aunt Candace moved the stairs and Alana got stuck in the upstairs corridor," I said. "She's telling everyone the library's full of hazards and I think they're arguing over who gets to include it in a book."

"Someone is going to come out of this with a hell of a

collection of weird stories," she remarked. "I guess it's a question of who gets there first. Otherwise there'll be lawsuits."

"Yeah, no kidding," I said. "Betsy isn't letting the murder accusation stop her from selling her marketing course to anyone who'll listen, and Beverly's still hunting for autographs, too. I'm starting to worry that we'll all lose our minds if they don't leave soon."

"There is that," she said. "But it's the library's reputation that worries me. We don't need a hundred guests spreading word throughout the magical world that we attract murderers."

My heart gave a twist of guilt. Even if our family wasn't the killer's direct targets, it'd make people think twice about using the library to host an event again. Estelle, as the head of social events, would heap all the blame on herself, which wasn't fair.

"I know," I said. "Worse, Laney didn't even smell anything at the crime scene except for—"

Before I could finish my sentence, a loud scream rose from behind us. I spun around, my heart sinking. "What's going on this time?"

Estelle and I ran to the Reading Corner, where Tiffany stood on top of a chair, her eyes wide as saucers. At first, I had no idea what she was staring at... then I saw a shadowy tentacle-like appendage withdraw under a nearby shelf.

"Is that a wraith?" said Estelle.

"Yes," I said. "I thought Cass was supposed to be in charge of catching that thing. How'd it get down here?"

She raised an eyebrow. "You left Cass to deal with it alone?"

"I thought she could handle it." I walked around the shelf, while Tiffany trembled on top of her chair. The other writers, true to form, had pulled out pens and paper ready to take notes. Only a couple of them had backed to a safe distance away. "She *told* me she didn't need help."

Estelle groaned. "Clearly, she bit off more than she could chew."

The door to the interview room flew open and Edwin walked out into the Reading Corner. "What is happening out here?"

"There's a monster!" Tiffany shrieked.

"Doesn't she know what it is?" I whispered to Estelle.

"Book wraiths aren't common outside of the library," she muttered back. "Blame Cass for encouraging them to move in here."

"Why am I not surprised it was her?"

We approached the shelf, but the shadow had already withdrawn from sight underneath. Estelle and I walked around the back and nearly collided with Aunt Candace coming the other way.

"Found your wraith, did you?" she said.

"Cass was supposed to be catching it,' I said. "I didn't know it'd escape and come downstairs. Any idea how to lure it out into the open?"

"Between the three of us, we can do it," Estelle said confidently. "Look—there it is."

I spotted a tentacle flicker into view and pulled out my wand, only for it to vanish from sight again. Crouching down, I aimed my wand under the shelf, but the gap was too narrow, and my freeze-frame spell bounced clean off the shelf. The second time, I cast a levitation charm and lifted the shelf slightly, firing off another freeze-frame spell immediately afterward.

"Did I hit it?" I asked the others.

"No," said Aunt Candace, whose eyes were glittering with amusement, her pen and notebook bouncing up and down at her side. "That thing is as slippery as smoke."

"Aunt Candace, stop writing and help us," said Estelle. "And where *is* Cass?"

"Wherever she is, the wraith sneaked out under her watch." I pointed my wand at the shelf again. "Or she got bored and went back to her animals."

A loud scream rose from nearby. I looked for the source and saw Haylee clinging to the hammock with her fingertips, while everyone backed slowly away from a shadowy tentacle inching from underneath the shelf behind her.

"How did it get over there?" I stepped in that direction.

"Shouldn't have moved the shelf, should you?" said Aunt Candace. "Wraiths can travel through shadows."

"That would have been nice to know earlier." I looked up as a feathery, winged shape passed overhead. "Sylvester, can you come and help me out?"

The owl ignored me, but a moment later, Cass ran over, her hair as wild as Aunt Candace's and her wand in her hand. "Where did it go?"

"Over there." Estelle walked alongside me to the spot where we'd seen the tentacle, having to dodge frantic guests in the process. "Don't make any sudden movements and it'll be less likely to run. How'd it escape you, Cass?"

She flicked her wand and a medium-sized metal cage slammed into the ground next to her. Her face was flushed with anger. "It jumped over the balcony before I could get it in this cage."

"I didn't know wraiths could jump," I commented.

"Maybe it really wanted to get into the Latin section," Sylvester called from above.

"Care to lend a hand?" I said to him.

"I don't have hands. I'm an owl."

Cass made a rude gesture at him and stalked towards the corner, levitating the cage alongside her. "Get out the way, everyone."

The crowd didn't move, so she pulled out her Biblio-Witch Inventory and hit a word. At once, everyone flew back as though pulled by invisible strings.

"Cass!" Estelle said in horrified tones, running to her side. "I'm sorry everyone—can you please stay back?"

Cass ignored her sister and waved her wand, and all the shelves in the vicinity leapt into the air as well. They floated around our heads, exposing a flat shadowy patch on the carpet.

Before any of us could move, the creature leapt into the air in a flash of shadowy tentacles and went *inside* the shelf instead.

"Cass, now look what you've done," said Estelle.

"Nobody asked your opinion," Cass shot back, with another flick of her wand which caused all the shelves to slam back into place with such intensity that the floor trembled and Tiffany fell off her chair.

"Cass, we need to lure it out," said Estelle.

"Jet," I called, and the little crow flew over to us. "Can you grab us a book from over in the ancient languages section, preferably something in Latin? And can you see the wraith from up there?"

"It's under there, partner!" squeaked Jet, zipping over a nearby shelf.

"Don't levitate it this time," said Estelle, to a grumbled reply from her sister. "Wait for Jet to get back with the bait and then we'll lure it out. Surround the shelves. I'll wait on this side and you and Rory can go over there."

Together, we made a sort of triangle formation around the shelf while Jet returned with a book of ancient languages. Not to be outdone, Sylvester swooped in and dropped no fewer than five leather-bound tomes onto the floor nearby.

"Wait!" I winced as several tentacles shot out from the shelf, one of them narrowly missing Jet.

"Partner!" he yelped.

"Hey!" I said. "Sylvester, stop dropping books on us. We have enough."

I pulled out my wand and levitated one of the books closer to the cage Cass had put on the ground.

Estelle did likewise. "If both of us keep moving the books around, can you manoeuvre the cage on top of the wraith, Cass?"

"Of course," she grunted. "Go on."

Between us, Estelle and I used magic to levitate the books around, forming a trail which led the tentacled creature along until it would have no choice but to leave the shelter of the bookshelves. Trying to ignore the sound of scribbling pens in the background, Estelle and I led the shadowy creature until its tentacles reached further and further out of the shelves. I levitated the biggest volume at an enticing distance from the shelf, and the book wraith finally scuttled into view.

"Now." Cass gave two flicks of her wand. At once, the

cage descended on top of the creature, trapping it on the floor.

Estelle and I moved in to help Cass seal the cage door. As we did so, the guests erupted into loud applause, interspersed with the sound of pens scribbling on paper. Even Cass looked mollified as she straightened upright.

"Show's over, folks," she said. "Get back to whatever you were doing."

"What's the betting that it shows up in a book within the year?" I whispered to Estelle.

"A year?" said Cass. "Try a month. Let me get that creature back upstairs before it slithers out of its cage again."

7

With the wraith restrained, Cass took the cage back upstairs single-handedly without listening to the guests' attempts to congratulate her on a feat well done. Sylvester didn't return either, perhaps miffed at our annoyance at him for throwing a mountain of textbooks at us.

That left it to Estelle and me to return the Reading Corner to its former state. Aunt Candace didn't seem inclined to lift a finger, while the guests weren't being much help, either. Tiffany, upon hopping off her chair, had marched off somewhere else to sulk. Alana offered to go after her, while Haylee glared at me. "Did you set that thing loose to terrify the killer into confessing?"

"No, it was an accident," I said. "It escaped on the floor above jumped over the balcony."

"What kind of circus is this?" she said.

"A magical library," I said, not particularly in the mood for another argument. "I'm sorry it attacked you, but we don't typically have long-term guests in here."

Estelle shot me a grateful look and then addressed the others. "I didn't expect the wraith to get loose in here. We usually keep that door locked, but given all the upheaval, it's been too chaotic for us to keep an eye on everything. It won't happen again."

"Never mind the wraith," said Haylee. "That cousin of yours was rude to all of us."

"Cass is under pressure, like we all are," Estelle said. "I *am* sorry she yelled at you, though."

Haylee sniffed. "I'm done here. It's pretty clear we aren't going to get a confession from the killer, and some of us have to get back home. I'm leaving."

She walked through the library towards the door, and Estelle and I hastened to follow her.

"You can't leave," Estelle protested. "If you do, Edwin and the police will have to take you into custody. Can you be patient for just a few hours?"

"Anywhere's better than here," she said, without turning back. "This is a waste of time anyway. It's only a matter of time before the police admit it and let me go."

"We found the scent of perfume at the crime scene," I told her. "The same perfume you were wearing yesterday."

That stopped her dead in her tracks. "What?"

Estelle shot me a look of surprise. I tried to figure out how to explain our discovery to Haylee without mentioning Laney's vampire status. "The people who looked at the crime scene said they smelled perfume in there. I remember it from earlier. It's hard to mistake."

"You went into Winona's room?" Estelle asked Haylee. "Before her death?"

"I didn't..." Haylee broke off. "I didn't kill her. I *did* go into her room, though. I went to check up on her this morning, but I thought she was asleep."

"Why'd you go to check up on her?" I asked.

"We argued last night," she said. "I wanted to apologise before everyone else woke up."

I raised an eyebrow. "So you walked into her room without knocking?"

"She's a heavy sleeper, especially when drunk," she said. "It didn't cross my mind that she might be dead. I'm innocent. I already told Edwin that."

I found myself wishing Laney was here to eavesdrop on her thoughts, because I was no expert in telling whether or not someone was lying. If she'd been close enough to Winona to leave the scent of her perfume at the scene, then I wasn't certain I believed her excuses.

"Well," I said, "it doesn't help your case when you lecture everyone in the library about the best way to hide a body."

"That wasn't me, it was Betsy," she said. "I thought she was the main suspect. The police should be taking her into custody once they're done with the questioning, right? They don't need to talk to me again."

"Only if you *told* them you checked up on Winona this morning," said Estelle. "When did you last see her alive?"

"At the party," she said promptly. "She went to bed after I did. I heard she was one of the last to leave the party, though Beverly stayed until the end. I don't think she even slept in her room."

"Really?" said Estelle. "She stayed downstairs all night?"

"I'm sure she did," said Haylee. "It wouldn't surprise me if she was the last to see Winona, if she remembers."

That was debatable. As drunk as she'd been last night, she might have no memory of anything which had occurred after the ceremony for all we knew. "All right, we'll speak to her."

While Haylee returned to the Reading Corner, I scanned the other guests. It looked like Tiffany and Alana were having a whispered argument, perhaps about the wraith, while Haylee sat down nearby and pulled out a notebook. I'd rather avoid questioning Beverly if I could help it, though if she'd been the last person who'd seen Winona alive, she ought to have mentioned it to the police, right?

A knock sounded from the front of the library. Estelle headed towards the door, while I followed close behind her. "Expecting someone?"

"I ordered catering from Zee's bakery for lunch," she said. "Figured it was the easiest way to feed our guests. Rory, can you get my mum? I'm going to need help getting everything in here. I think she's still helping Edwin's assistant to examine the body."

"Sure." I walked over to the classroom adjacent to the one Edwin had picked out for the questioning and knocked on the door. "Aunt Adelaide?"

My aunt opened the door. "The catering showed up, did it?"

"Yeah," I said. "Estelle and I had to stop Haylee from walking out of the library, so I hope this distracts everyone."

"Tell me about it later," she said. "I'll be right behind you."

We spent the next half-hour levitating boxes of food onto the hastily conjured buffet tables near the Reading

Corner, while Edwin returned to the police station to speak to the other staff about whether they'd had any luck with questioning the guests at the hotel. At least the supplies from Zee's bakery somewhat distracted everyone from the aftermath of the book wraith's attack, though I saw Tiffany liberally dipping into the bottle of wine someone had brought out from among the winners' prizes.

I grabbed a muffin and settled behind the front desk to eat it while I updated Aunt Adelaide on the events of the morning. She shook her head and tutted when I told her about Cass and the wraith.

"I knew I shouldn't have left her to deal with it on her own," I said. "In fairness, none of us knew the wraith could jump over the balcony. I also didn't know wraiths were so little-known even in the magical world. Did Cass bring them to the library?"

"Actually, it was our mother... your grandmother, Rory," she replied. "She had a soft spot for vulnerable animals."

"Wait, that's where Cass got her attachment to magical creatures?" I finished my muffin and tossed the wrapper into the bin. "I didn't know rescuing kelpies ran in the family."

"I don't think your grandmother ever rescued a kelpie," commented Aunt Adelaide.

"Guess I learn something new every day," I said. "Cass probably won't be coming back downstairs. Have you figured out what Winona was poisoned with yet?"

"No," she said. "With no evidence from the crime scene, we can only assume Winona was poisoned before she went upstairs."

"Yeah, the only thing Laney smelled in her room was Haylee's perfume, but Haylee is denying any involvement," I said. "She told us she went up there to check on Winona this morning and apologise for some argument they had, but she didn't realise she was dead at the time."

"Is that what she claims?" said Aunt Adelaide.

"She insists she's innocent, which naturally makes me more suspicious," I admitted. "She also tried to leave the library after the wraith's escape, but Estelle and I managed to convince her to come back in."

"Estelle is handling this as well as she can, considering," said Aunt Adelaide. "She doesn't need to beat herself up about it."

"Neither do you," I added. "It's not your fault either. What's happening with the guests at the hotel?"

"Edwin will come back with an update, I imagine," she said. "The tricky part is narrowing down who might have had contact with Winona last night."

"Because pretty much everyone did," I said. "And half of them were drunk enough that they might not have noticed anything out of place. What about people who personally knew Winona, then?"

"Again… that's everyone here," she said. "She was chosen to host the event for a reason. If they didn't like her, they didn't have to show up."

"Exactly." Estelle walked over, looking frazzled. "The only person who openly complained was Haylee, and I get the impression she's a serial complainer. She wants everything run her way."

"Wasn't there a rumour about Haylee bribing other people into voting for her?" I said.

"I forgot about that," said Estelle. "Not sure it implicates her as guilty in a murder, though."

"Might be worth checking out."

Estelle shook her head. "I'd have to dig deep into an online search to find out, and there's no time. Might just be a rumour, anyway."

"True," I said. "What about Beverly, then? Haylee implied she was probably the last person to leave the party. Do you think it's worth asking her if she saw anything?"

"I guess," said Estelle. "I wish I'd stayed at the party until the end, but I was exhausted. I left Winona to deal with the rest, to tell you the truth."

"So did I." Aunt Adelaide exhaled in a sigh. "We all made mistakes, but—oh, there's Edwin."

The elf policeman had entered the library again, and Aunt Adelaide swept over to him.

"Any updates?" she asked.

"We've decided to move the questioning to the police station," he said. "I've gathered a list of suspects I'd like to talk to again, if that's okay."

"Sure, go ahead," said Estelle.

Aunt Adelaide and I followed the elf policeman back to the Reading Corner, where the guests all looked warily at Edwin as he approached them. Except for Tiffany, who'd dozed off on a bean bag with an empty wine glass dangling from her hand, and Beverly, who'd commandeered the hammock. Anticipation rippled through the crowd as everyone waited to see who'd landed themselves near the top of the suspect list.

"Would the following individuals please come with me," said Edwin.

He then read off a list of names. Betsy Blake and Haylee Grace were both on the list, to no surprise. Outraged exclamations broke out among the guests, and the noise caused Beverly to startle awake from her nap. She immediately sprang to her feet. "Are you arresting Betsy? And Haylee?"

"No," said Edwin. "However, I am asking them to come with me to the police station for further questioning."

"No!" She ran to Betsy's side. "You can't arrest them. What happens if she can't finish the next book in the series?"

"Someone's priorities are in the right place, aren't they?" I muttered to Aunt Adelaide.

She clucked her tongue. "I'd better go and help Edwin, I think."

At least Beverly was awake now, so I could speak to her about what she might have seen at the end of the party. First, though, I had to wait for the others to leave. Aunt Adelaide and Edwin talked to Haylee, who was protesting loudly, while Betsy looked like she was about to pass out. I had to agree that the best idea was to take the most likely suspects into custody. If nothing else, we'd all feel more secure here in the library with a lower chance of anyone else getting murdered.

Supervised by Aunt Adelaide, their group left the library, and everything grew considerably quieter. I scanned the area and spotted Aunt Candace slinking away towards the living quarters.

I made my way over to her. "You're not sneaking off to work on your book, are you?"

She looked affronted. "Would it be a crime if I was? I'm not a suspect, am I?"

"No," I said, "but we could use your help around the library. Most of the guests are still here."

"I would prefer to avoid Beverly pestering me to write another book in the series I finished six years ago," she said. "She also keeps trying to persuade me to drop hints about everything I'm working on."

"Speaking of Beverly, she was also the last person to leave the party, allegedly," I said. "I'm wondering if she saw the killer at any point in the night."

"*Was* she, now?" she said. "How interesting."

"Yeah," I said. "I thought we could speak to her. I feel like she's more likely to listen to you than to me, though."

"Only if I bribed her with information on my next book," she said. "Which I'm not inclined to do."

I raised an eyebrow. "It's up to you. I don't think she killed Winona, but she might have been one of the last people to see her alive. Not sure she will have mentioned that to Edwin, though."

"No, I suppose not." She pursed her lips. "I suppose I *might* drop a hint or two…"

"Might get her to leave you alone for the rest of the day," I added.

Her expression cleared. "Then I'll do it."

She strode back towards the Reading Corner with a great air of self-importance, as though she'd volunteered to go to war and not to deal with an overeager fan. We didn't need to corner Beverly, though, because the instant she saw us, she sprang over to Aunt Candace. "There you are. Have you decided to think about continuing your Sunny Valley mystery series yet?"

"Yes," said Aunt Candace. "I have too many other

projects in the queue, but I'll keep it in mind. My next series is going to be set in the same universe."

Beverly's face lit up. "Really? I loved that series. Have you thought about—" And she launched into a long diatribe which was largely incomprehensible to me.

Aunt Candace's expression grew more and more discomfited, so I interjected when Beverly stopped to breathe. "Hey, Beverly. I heard you were the last to leave the party, and I wondered if you saw anyone acting oddly?"

She blinked. "Like that weird creature which attacked Tiffany?"

"No, people," I said. "Was Winona the last person to go to bed?"

"I think so," she said. "I asked her if I could take a look at her new book and she said no. I was drunk at the time, so I don't remember much."

"New book?" I echoed. "Was she working on something new?"

"Yes, I think she was," she said vaguely. "I don't think Betsy killed her, you know. She was so drunk last night that Haylee had to levitate her up to her room. I went along to make sure she got there in one piece."

"She didn't mention that earlier," I said.

That might account for how her perfume had got everywhere, but not how it'd ended up in Winona's room.

"It's hardly news," said Aunt Candace in unimpressed tones. "Haylee is as much of a compulsive liar as Betsy is. Comes in handy when writing stories, but it's a nuisance the rest of the time."

"What do you think of Haylee?" I asked Beverly. "Did

she and Winona know one another well? I heard they had an argument last night."

"Oh, they did," she said. "I think it was about Winona's next book. Speaking of, will it be published? Do you know?"

"I haven't a clue," Aunt Candace replied. "I imagine it'll be up to her family."

And with that, she extricated herself from the conversation and escaped the Reading Corner, leaving me alone with Beverly.

"I don't think Haylee killed anyone either," Beverly supplied. "She's working on fifteen different series, you know. Why would she risk everything she's built?"

"I don't know," I said. "Ah... is it true that she might have bribed people into voting for her?"

"Who said that?" said Beverly. "That's horrible."

"Just a rumour," I said, wishing I'd looked up where it'd come from before mentioning it. "Did she desperately want to win the prize?"

"Everyone wanted to win," she said. "So, what's it like being the Lost Cousin? Your aunt wrote your dad's story into a book, right? How does that feel?"

"Uh... weird." I looked around for an escape and caught sight of Laney near the corridor to the living quarters. "Gotta go—I need to talk to my friend."

I made my escape to the living quarters, where Laney raised her eyebrows at me. "What're you running from?"

"Beverly," I said. "I wanted to find out if she was really the last person to leave the party last night, but she evaded our questions and started pestering us, so I had to escape before she talked my ear off."

"She was the last to leave the party?" said Laney. "You don't think she saw the killer, do you?"

"I honestly don't think she'd accuse anyone here even if she saw them do it," I admitted. "She hero-worships every author in the room."

"Including your Aunt Candace," she said. "This is going well, isn't it?"

"How're you holding up, anyway?" I asked. "I thought you were going to take a nap."

"There's too much noise," she said. "Besides, I don't want to sleep through the action."

"Not much action happening in here." Though I wouldn't be able to rest easily with a killer potentially on the loose, either.

"True." She fidgeted. "I wish I could hear their thoughts. I did try, you know, but I didn't pick up on any real hints."

"Don't worry about it," I said. "We need some concrete evidence, but even the library doesn't have a room which'll summon up the answers."

Or did it? One room in the library theoretically contained the answers to any question, but the Forbidden Room came with its own set of risks. There was also a good chance it wouldn't give us any useful information, either, but at this point, anything was worth trying.

8

I would have dug out the Book of Questions there and then, but when I went back to the front desk, it was to find Edwin waiting there with an expectant look on his face.

"Anything new?" I asked. "Betsy and Haylee didn't give you any trouble, did they?"

"No, but they're to remain in custody until they've been questioned again," he said. "They're also telling me stories about a shadow attacking people. What's been going on in here?"

"A book wraith got loose," I explained to him. "We managed to recapture it, and nobody was hurt."

"How did I guess something like that would happen?" he said.

"It's a hazard of holding everyone here in the library," I said. "The guests getting restless and wandering out of bounds, too."

"I can't say I'm surprised," he said. "Ah—there's Gregor."

The wizard walked over to us, while Aunt Adelaide followed close behind him with a grim expression on her face.

"We identified the poison used on the victim," said the wizard. "When dissolved in water, it becomes colourless and impossible to identify except by its distinct scent. It's also fairly slow-acting, taking several hours to take effect."

"So there's a good chance someone gave it to her at the party," I concluded. "Is there anything left from the party itself, or did you clear the place out?"

"I cleared everything up," said Aunt Adelaide. "If there was any evidence lying around, there isn't any longer."

"It's okay," I said. "You couldn't have known."

"Exactly," said Edwin. "At this point, we have a good idea of last night's events. What we're lacking is a motive."

"Betsy certainly has one," I said. "Haylee, I don't know, but she and Winona did have some kind of argument last night."

"I'm fairly sure everyone here has argued with everyone else at least once," commented Aunt Adelaide. "Edwin, what about the guests at the hotel?"

"We've questioned them all," he said. "Most of them aren't closely acquainted with any of the nominees. I've struck a good deal of them off the list on the grounds that they didn't know the victim, and I think it's more likely to be one of the other authors than not."

Yeah, I thought so. "So it's more likely to be Haylee, Betsy, or someone else who was staying here at the library?"

"Precisely," said Aunt Adelaide. "I saw you talking to Beverly earlier. Did she have anything to say?"

"She mentioned Betsy was so drunk last night that she

passed out early and had to be levitated up to her room," I said. "Haylee was the one who levitated her up there, too. Not sure Betsy would have been able to commit murder while unconscious, unless she administered the poison earlier."

Edwin's brow furrowed. "I will go back and talk to both of them. Gregor, bring the body with you to the police station. The others will stay here in the library for now."

As he left, I heard wings beating overhead. Perhaps Sylvester had more to add to my impression of last night's events. He'd had a bird's eye view of the event, literally, and he hadn't been distracted or intoxicated. He also happened to have access to a part of the library that few others did. The place which supposedly had all the answers. Not that it'd been much help on other occasions, but maybe this time it would provide some much-needed insight.

"Do you think the Forbidden Room might be able to shed some light on the situation?" I asked Aunt Adelaide.

"Maybe," she replied, "but you'd have to ask the right question. You only get one chance per day."

We each get one chance, technically. But the Forbidden Room was notorious for giving answers which weren't particularly helpful and leaving us at a loose end. It was the owl who controlled the Forbidden Room, after all, and so far, I was the only person who actually knew Sylvester's secret. Now did not seem the best time to inform the rest of my family of that fact, especially with Sylvester himself unsettled by the presence of so many strangers in the library. However, I couldn't think of a better way to find the missing evidence than to consult the Book of Questions.

"You don't have to stay here and watch the desk, Rory," said Aunt Adelaide. "Take a break and practise magic or read a book."

Or my dad's journal. Yet my curiosity over the journal had almost been overshadowed by the lingering question of who'd poisoned Winona, and if I wanted a chance at getting any peace to read the journal again, I needed to do my part to help solve the mystery. "Okay, I'll see you in a bit."

I did have a pile of reading to do for my magical theory classes, but that could wait. Instead, I looked around for Sylvester and spotted him perching on the balcony of the first floor. I climbed the stairs and approached him from behind. "Hey, Sylvester."

"How did I guess you'd come looking for me?" Instead of turning around, Sylvester did that creepy thing where he rotated his head and not his body, his owl-eyes looking me up and down. "What is it? Need another favour? Has your friend set something else loose?"

"Did *you* know the wraith could jump over the balcony?" I asked.

"Certainly not," he said. "If your friend doesn't keep her nose out of those rooms, I'll put a mouse in her bed."

"Come on, you know it was an accident," I said. "Putting all that aside, if you want the guests to leave the library, we're going to have to solve this case. Would the Forbidden Room be able to help us unearth the evidence of who poisoned Winona?"

"I already told you the Forbidden Room can't answer questions like that," he said.

"But this time, the murder *did* happen in the library," I pointed out. "And we haven't been able to find any evidence. We know the cause of death but not where the poison came from, or where it ended up."

He clucked his beak. "I don't know why you're complaining to me. If you want to ask a question, go ahead and pick up the book."

"Will it actually help?" Maybe it really was that simple, but the Room never gave anything away for free. Especially evidence which might solve a murder.

The owl, typically, didn't deign to answer, so I waited for Aunt Adelaide to move away from the front desk before I headed down and picked the Book of Questions out of its usual place behind the counter. The book's cover was made of black leather and totally blank except for a silver question mark on the spine. I definitely didn't want the guests getting wind of what I was up to, so I went into the family's living quarters for some privacy.

The cover of the book sparkled faintly as it caught the light, and I drew in a deep breath before flipping it open and saying, "I wish to enter the Forbidden Room."

At once, I fell, tumbling head over heels into the air as the pages shifted and drew me into their embrace. My cloak spun over my head while I tumbled down, falling headfirst into a small room with black-painted walls.

I landed on my knees, the soft carpet breaking my fall. I looked up, dizzy and disorientated as I usually was when I fell into the Forbidden Room. Then I climbed to my feet shakily, readying my question.

"Will you give me evidence pointing to the person who murdered Winona Clair?"

A flash engulfed the room, and I screwed up my eyes

against the glare before opening them again. Lying opposite me was a bound heap of paper and nothing more. While I knew Sylvester must be watching from somewhere inside the room, I might as well have been alone.

I crossed the room and examined the papers. Winona's name was printed on the top. Was this a copy of the manuscript she'd been working on?

"How did this end up in here?" I asked the room in general.

No response came.

"Sylvester?" I called out. "Where was this before you brought it here? Did the killer hide it?"

Or were the answers in the manuscript itself? I flipped to the next page, but it would take all day to read the whole book, and besides, the fact that it'd turned up in the room at all meant it must count as evidence. Unless Sylvester was trying to reprimand me for trying to cheat my way to the answers, which was a possibility.

Without warning, the floor fell out from underneath me once again. I tumbled out of the room, gripping the manuscript in my hands, and landed flat on my back in the Reading Corner.

For a moment, I lay still, breathless. Then I sat up and noticed everyone in the vicinity was staring at me. *Uh-oh.* I climbed to my feet as Beverly bounded over to me, peering at the manuscript. "Isn't that Winona's manuscript?"

"Where did you get that?" asked Alana Flower.

I couldn't exactly tell them about the Forbidden Room, so I said, "Upstairs in the library. Someone left it lying around."

"It's Winona's," said Alana. "Did she leave it somewhere before she died?"

"No clue." Sylvester wouldn't have given me the manuscript if it wasn't important, but why had he decided to drop me in front of an audience? "Didn't the police search her bags?"

"They searched all our bags," said one of the others. "The police wouldn't have known she brought the manuscript with her, not if it went missing before she died."

Several others murmured agreement. Everyone was staring at me, except for Tiffany, who'd somehow slept through the whole thing. I suspected the empty wine glass in her hand might have had something to do with it.

"Did anyone here know Winona brought the manuscript with her?" I asked the group. "Because she might not have been the one who hid it."

I scanned the others' faces, noting that Beverly's gaze darted from me to the manuscript and back again as though she was trying to avoid my eyes.

"I knew she was working on it," she ventured. "Not that she brought it with her."

Hmm.

"Anyone else know anything?" I asked.

Nobody answered. I looked around for the Book of Questions, which had landed on the floor beside me, and picked it up, tucking it underneath my arm.

Estelle walked over and saw the bound manuscript in my hands. "Rory, what is that?"

"It's Winona's manuscript." I hurried to join her, out of earshot of the others, and held up the Book of Questions with my free hand. "I found it when I was looking for evidence."

Her eyes bulged, realising my implication. "Someone stole it? But... did they do it before or after her death?"

"Precisely," I said. "Nobody will admit to anything."

But what about the others who'd gone with Edwin to the police station for further questioning? If one of them had taken and hidden the manuscript, then we wouldn't know unless we asked them, too.

"I'll call and tell Edwin," said Estelle, as though she'd sensed the direction of my thoughts. "Can you watch the others? I'll send my mum to help you out if she's around."

"Sure," I said, though the last thing I wanted was for everyone to realise I'd used the library's magic to transport myself straight to the evidence. Not just because that might give the murderer a new target, but I didn't want everyone to know the Book of Questions existed. Sylvester would not be thrilled if certain guests figured out the secret magic we had hidden in the library.

Sure enough, it didn't take long before Beverly approached me again. "Can I read the manuscript?"

"I'm afraid we have to give it to the police, since it's evidence," I said. "Edwin will be on his way..."

Thankfully, Aunt Adelaide showed up at that moment to rescue me. "Estelle said you found Winona's missing manuscript?"

"That's right." I held it up. "Where should I put it until Edwin gets here?"

"I'll take it." She held out a hand. "No, Beverly, you can't take it to the police. Where—" She broke off, glancing at the Book of Questions underneath my arm. "I'll take that, too."

"I'll lock up the manuscript," I added, seizing on an excuse to duck out of sight of the others. Specifically, Beverly. "Estelle is calling Edwin, so I'll put it in the room he was using for questioning."

Before I left, Aunt Adelaide leaned in and whispered, "Did the Room give it to you?"

"Yes, but I don't know where it was," I whispered back. "I asked for evidence pointing to the killer, but there was no explanation."

"I thought as much," she said. "Lock it up until Edwin gets here."

"All right." I made my way through the stacks, going on a roundabout route to avoid walking directly through the Reading Corner. Once I was sure nobody was behind me, I located the classroom and put the manuscript inside it. Then I waved my wand on the closed door and cast a locking charm on it.

After checking the room was secure, I walked back around the outskirts of the Reading Corner. As I did so, a gasp rose from among the guests, followed by a series of shocked whispers. I poked my head out between the shelves, curious, and spotted Xavier nearby. His scythe was out, wreathed in an odd ethereal glow. Which had only one cause.

"Oh, no," I said. "Who...?"

My gaze followed his to the body of Tiffany Wren, Aunt Candace's ex-cowriter, who occupied the same bean bag as she had before. I'd thought she was napping, but she hadn't moved in hours, and only now did I notice how very still she was.

"I thought she was asleep," someone said.

"Me too," said Alana in a hushed voice, her gaze darting to the Reaper with a mixture of awe and fear.

I looked between Xavier and Tiffany's body, my heart sinking in my chest. "Did you already reap her soul?"

"I did," he confirmed. "She didn't know she was dead."

This was going to cause problems.

9

There followed a confusing few minutes of questions and accusations as we waited for Edwin to return to the library and Aunt Adelaide ordered everyone to stay put in order to make sure nobody else was unaccounted for. Estelle waited for Edwin while Xavier and I kept a close eye on the restless guests.

"How long was she dead for?" I whispered to Xavier. Had she already been dead before Edwin had escorted Haylee and Betsy out of the library? I found myself wishing I'd checked on her earlier, but everyone had thought she was sleeping. Except, it seemed, for the killer.

"Only a few minutes," said Xavier. "Do you think the poison was the same as the one used on the other victim?"

"If it was, the poison takes several hours to take effect," I said. "According to my Aunt Adelaide, anyway. But it must have taken longer to affect Winona if she drank it last night."

Did that mean it wasn't the same poison? Even if it

was, it took long enough to take effect that anyone might have given it to Tiffany, even someone from among the group of people Edwin had taken to the police station for further questioning. Which didn't help us narrow down the list any further.

"Maybe the dose was higher with Tiffany, if she drank the whole bottle herself," he commented. "That's just guesswork, though. Who would have picked now to target her?"

"It's got to be someone who was jealous of her win," I said to him. "Why else would they target both her and Winona? That's the only link between the two of them."

But if Betsy and Haylee were in the clear, then we were back at square one again.

"I wouldn't know," said Xavier. "I wish the police had agreed to let everyone stay somewhere that wasn't the library."

"They took away the main suspects to stay in police custody, but I think they acted too late," I said. "Did Tiffany say anything to you when you took her to the afterlife?"

"No," he said. "She was surprised to be dead."

I thought back to the confused hour after the book wraith's escape. "Where'd her wine glass go? She was drinking from one earlier, and there might be traces of the poison left inside it. Nobody was paying any attention at the time."

Which was no doubt what the killer had been counting on.

The library door opened, and Edwin walked in, accompanied by the same troll guards from earlier along with his wizard assistant. Aunt Adelaide beckoned Gregor through into the room where she'd taken the body, while Edwin and the trolls approached the guests in the Reading Corner.

"Who was the last person to speak to Tiffany Wren?" the elf policeman asked the gathering guests.

Nobody spoke for a long moment.

"I saw her working on her book," Alana ventured. "Then I assumed she fell asleep."

"I saw her at the buffet table," someone else added. "Was that where she was poisoned?"

"Are we all going to die?" said Beverly tremulously.

Good question.

"No, of course not," said Estelle, striding over. "The buffet carts were checked thoroughly before being brought in. There was nothing wrong with the food."

Panicked shouts and questions fired back and forth across the Reading Corner.

"Wasn't she drinking from a wine glass?" I had to raise my voice to be heard. "Whose wine was it? It didn't come from the buffet carts."

"Must have been left over from the party," Estelle said, looking pale. "Maybe... stop panicking, everyone. It won't help. Most poison is quick acting enough that it would already have killed everyone intended to be the targets. Nobody else is missing, are they?"

"No," said Edwin. "We took a register. Everyone is here except for those selected to be questioned further. Tell me where you last saw her, however mundane. Any detail might help."

"Right there," said Alana, pointing at the bean bag. "Thought she was asleep."

Several people murmured agreement. Nobody could

confirm when Tiffany had last been alive, but everyone had been here the whole time. The killer had poisoned her in plain sight.

"What does the Reaper have to say?" asked Beverly. "Did you speak to Tiffany's ghost?"

Everyone turned in Xavier's direction. *Oh, no.*

"She had nothing to say," he said to the others. "She couldn't identify her killer. If she was poisoned without knowing, it's not a surprise."

"But what if we're *all* poisoned?" said Beverly. "Do you have an antidote?"

"That's enough," Edwin said. "Beverly—you'll come with me for questioning first."

The guests broke into protests, while Estelle walked among them, trying to calm their fervour. While I had to admit that they had a point—for all we knew, there *had* been more than one target for the poison—Aunt Adelaide put that theory to bed when she walked over with her wand in her hand.

"I'll use a poison-detecting spell on all of you," she said. "Will that assuage your fears?"

"Yes!" said Alana.

They crowded around Aunt Adelaide, while Xavier and I backed out of range. From what I heard, though, it sounded like poor Tiffany had been the only victim of the poison this time around.

"Question is, where'd the wine itself disappear to?" I asked. "Unless it disappeared with the leftovers from the buffet tables…"

"We'll find it," said Estelle. "We'll have a proper look around the Reading Corner once the guests are out of the way."

"I should go," said Xavier. "I need to tell my boss."

"Sure." I walked with him to the door, relieved to get away from the agitated guests. "Sorry about Beverly. I was a little worried she might try to get *your* autograph next."

"Would that be a bad thing?" he said. "Or am I not famous enough?"

I grinned despite myself. "Only with me."

"And you'd rather not share?" He slipped his hand into mine, and I found myself seriously considering walking out of there with him and leaving the guests to their arguments. Except I'd rather not speak to the Grim Reaper, and I couldn't forget the reason he'd come to the library to begin with.

"No, but this isn't a good time to be famous," I said. "I mean, Tiffany and Winona were only well-known in certain circles and I don't think they had any weird internet stalkers, but who knows."

"Tiffany was poisoned in public," said Xavier. "That definitely feels personal."

"I wonder if they poisoned the wine when the book wraith got loose," I said. "Everyone was distracted, and the entire Reading Corner got upended in the process."

Xavier's brows shot up. "Wait, the book wraith got out again?"

"Laney accidentally left the door to the Vampire Section open," I said. "It's been one disaster after another in here."

"You do seem to be besieged with bad luck," he said. "Do you think the same person killed both victims?"

"Has to be," I said. "But they waited until everyone was distracted before striking again. Worse, we don't know if the poison was given to her by someone who was already taken to the police station or not. If we knew, we might be able to narrow it down."

"Edwin took the main suspects, right?" he said. "Might it have been one of them?"

"Betsy is still a suspect," I said. "Though Haylee did have an argument with Winona... oh, no. Aunt Candace is upstairs, and she doesn't know what happened down here."

Worse, she and Tiffany had once been friends and co-writers. I didn't want to think about how she'd react when we told her Tiffany was dead.

"Ah," he said. "I suppose you'll have to tell her eventually, though."

That's the problem. "Yeah. You should go back to your boss. If he wants to come here in person, then tell him there are a bunch of writers looking for new material for their books."

He grinned. "That'll put him off. I'll see you soon."

He gave me a quick hug and kiss goodbye. Once he'd left, I made my way back to the Reading Corner and tracked down Estelle.

"We should move everyone somewhere else so we can search the crime scene," I said in a low voice. "Get them into one of the other classrooms or something."

"I thought about that, but they'd have to be supervised," she said. "I should have known taking away the main suspects wouldn't be enough to assure the others' safety."

"We couldn't have known the killer would have the audacity to strike again so soon," I reminded her. "If anything, they're more likely to have left evidence behind. What about the wine glass Tiffany was drinking out of?

And the bottle itself? It couldn't have disappeared into thin air."

"I know." She turned to one of the troll guards. "Can you help us move everyone into a classroom?"

The others obeyed with surprisingly minimal fuss, even Beverly. Once the Reading Corner was clear, we began our search. Unfortunately, the whole place had been upended during the fight with the wraith and none of the chairs or bean bags were in the same places they'd previously been in. The chaos would certainly have afforded the killer an opportunity to slip some poison into Tiffany's wine.

I finally tracked down the bean bag where Tiffany had sat and crouched down beside it. Underneath lay a discarded wine glass, with the merest trace of liquid in the bottom.

"Here it is." I beckoned Estelle over. "Should we hand it to the police?"

"My mum's talking to Gregor in the spare room." She took the glass from me. "I'll take it to her."

As she walked away, I did another circuit of the Reading Corner and halted near the spot where the buffet tables had been standing. A classroom door stood slightly open in front of me, and a gleaming light shone from within the room.

The trophy. I pushed the door open and slipped inside, finding the winner's prize sitting unattended in the room. Magically conjured birds flew in half-hearted circles around the trophy, an envelope sat on the desk... and beside it were two bottles of wine.

I crossed the room and picked up both bottles, taking them to the room where Estelle stood talking to Aunt

Adelaide and Gregor. Poor Tiffany's body lay on a table behind them.

"Where'd these come from?" I held up the bottles. "They were with the winners' prizes."

Estelle clapped a hand to her mouth. "Winona gave Tiffany a bottle of wine to go with her trophy. I saw her at the party yesterday."

"Did she now?" said Gregor.

"Of course," said Aunt Adelaide. "I forgot."

"One of the bottles might contain the poison," I said. "Maybe the whole bottle was poisoned, not Tiffany's wine glass. It'd explain how they got it in here without anyone suspecting."

"Winona brought the bottle, though?" said Estelle. "She didn't poison it herself, did she?"

"The poison might've been slipped into the bottle while the party was going on," I commented. "Maybe she and Tiffany were both the targets, but for whatever reason, Tiffany didn't end up drinking from the right bottle yesterday."

That was pure guesswork, but it made more sense than most of the other theories I'd come up with.

"I'll check both." Aunt Adelaide raised her wand. "Nobody else showed signs of being poisoned when I used my detection spell. This was personal."

As I thought.

A glow spread from her wand to the bottles. One glowed blue around the edges, and the other took on a red hue.

"That's the one," Aunt Adelaide said softly. "It's half empty. No wonder it acted so much quicker on Tiffany than it did on Winona."

"I'll have to take this." Gregor stepped in and claimed the bottle. "Are you sure nobody else drank any of it?"

"We'll check with the guests," said Estelle. "But I doubt your spell was faulty, Mum. It was just Tiffany who was the target."

We left the classroom and made our way to the guests' new spot in one of the other adjacent rooms. I could hear the scratching of pens from behind the door, indicating that at least someone was trying to get a good story out of this new development. Aunt Candace, however, had yet to come down to see what was going on. Cass, too, though the latter wasn't a particular surprise.

"Who's going to fetch Aunt Candace?" I asked Estelle. "Someone has to tell her."

"I know." She bit her lower lip. "That might turn ugly. More than it already is, I mean."

"Yeah," I murmured. "I can go and tell her, if you like. Or I can ask the guests about the wine. You pick one and I'll pick the other. Then we'll get both over with."

"Someone needs to tell Cass, too," she said. "Where's Sylvester?"

"Upstairs, last I saw," I said. "I doubt he'll help us out, though. He's not exactly going to fall over himself to volunteer to give bad news to Aunt Candace."

"Fair point," she said. "I'll deal with the guests, if you don't mind speaking to Aunt Candace."

I nodded. "Might as well get it over with before she finds out herself and gets mad at us for not telling her first."

"Thanks, Rory," Estelle said. "I'll make it up to you, promise."

"Don't worry about it." Aunt Candace had been in an

agreeable mood earlier, but that would doubtless change when she learned of Tiffany's death. Regardless, it was probably best to come out with it directly rather than waiting until later. The guests weren't leaving anytime soon, after all.

While Estelle went to talk to her mother, I made my way to our family's living quarters and climbed the stairs to the very top, where a wooden door led to Aunt Candace's private room. I knocked on the door and waited for Aunt Candace to answer. When no response came, I knocked again.

"What?" came Aunt Candace's muffled voice from the other side.

"It's Rory," I said. "Um, something else happened downstairs. We need you."

The door inched open a crack. "Go bother someone else."

"You have to know this." I squashed my instincts to take the opportunity to leave before the inevitable happened. "It's important."

The door opened another inch or two. "Why?"

"It's Tiffany," I said. "She was poisoned, just like Winona."

"What?"

I took a step back as the door flew wide and Aunt Candace stormed past me down the stairs, nearly bowling me over in the process.

"Aunt Candace!" I hastened to follow her downstairs, but there was no stopping her. She stomped all the way down three flights of stairs and into the main part of the library, without pausing for breath until she reached the Reading Corner.

Aunt Adelaide moved to intercept her sister. "Candace—"

"Who killed Tiffany?" she demanded. "Where's the body?"

"She was poisoned a couple of hours ago," Aunt Adelaide said calmly. "The body is in the classroom with Gregor, but we already know it was poison that killed her. Someone poisoned the bottle of wine Winona gave her as her prize."

Aunt Candace's face flushed like a traffic light. "*Betsy.* She slipped in the poison last night, the crafty menace."

"Do calm down, Candace." Aunt Adelaide coaxed her shocked sister over to an armchair. "We're doing all we can to find the perpetrator, but it won't help anyone if you start getting hysterical."

"I know it was Betsy Blake," she said. "I demand to speak to her right now, if none of you will."

"Candace!" said Aunt Adelaide. "We'll find out who did it, but if you don't let the police do their jobs, it'll take longer than it needs to."

"We're wasting time," Aunt Candace insisted. "We already know who the killer is."

"We don't know for sure," I said. "Tiffany died after Betsy and the others were already taken to the police station for further questioning. Granted, the poison might have been put into the wine before then, but if not, it might have been someone else after all."

"Betsy was jealous of her win from the start," Aunt Candace said. "I hope she spends the rest of her life behind bars."

"We'll figure it out," said Aunt Adelaide. "For now, I'd try not to upset the others. They're trapped here for the duration, knowing there's a potential murderer among their number."

"So are we, and we live here," she said. "Tiffany and I might not always have seen eye to eye, but I won't let her murderer wander around here unchecked. If Edwin even thinks about letting Betsy go..."

"Is there the smallest chance the murder might not have had anything to do with Tiffany winning the prize?" I said. "Because I'm not sure poisoning the whole bottle would have been an efficient way to get the right person."

"If it was Tiffany's gift, then she wouldn't have shared it with anyone," said Aunt Candace confidently. "I'm guessing Betsy didn't intend her to drop dead here in the library."

"I suppose nobody else was drinking wine in the middle of the day," I allowed. "But the reason she was drinking is because she got scared half to death by that wraith."

Which, in a roundabout way, put the blame back on my family again. From the grim look on Aunt Adelaide's face, the same thought had occurred to her.

"First Winona and now this," Aunt Candace muttered. "Of course it was Betsy. Who else would it be?"

"Well, for one thing, I went to ask the Book of Questions for evidence of the killer and the manuscript Winona was working on showed up inside the room," I said. "I think someone hid it, possibly the killer, but that doesn't have anything to do with the award, does it? Why would Betsy take Winona's manuscript?"

Aunt Candace looked at me for a moment. "I have no idea."

She sounded shaken, and I didn't blame her a bit. She'd

had a serious shock. But I couldn't help feeling like I'd missed another connection somewhere. If the killer was angry at not winning the prize, why take the manuscript Winona was working on? The two had nothing to do with one another. It wasn't like Winona herself had been nominated for the prize.

Aunt Candace, however, refused to be deterred. She waited until Edwin came out of the room where he'd been questioning the people still in the library, and then pounced on him. "Where are you going?"

"To talk to the suspects at the police station," he said. "I'm going to ask them to explain what they were doing at the time of Tiffany's death and use the clues to inform both investigations."

"Not without me, you aren't," she said. "If Betsy was the one who killed Tiffany, I'm the one she'll have to deal with next."

"That isn't appropriate," said Edwin.

"Tiffany was my cowriter," Aunt Candace said in heated tones. "Betsy knows I'll ruin her if I find her guilty. She'll spill everything when I ask her to, mark my words."

Edwin shook his head, but I could see his resolve weakening. Spending the day dealing with Aunt Candace and the others had probably worn him down, and this second murder was the last straw. On the other hand, letting Aunt Candace loose in the police station without supervision did not strike me as a wise move. I gave Aunt Adelaide a look, asking her if it was okay to go along with her. She responded with a faint nod, giving me permission.

"Edwin, I'll come, too," I said. "I'll watch out for trouble."

Edwin exhaled. "All right, but I won't have you antagonising the other prisoners *or* my staff. That clear, Candace?"

"Clear as a polished cauldron," she said sourly.

Looked like it was up to me to keep her in line. I followed close behind Edwin as Aunt Candace stormed out of the library as though she was being pursued by the Grim Reaper himself. My second thoughts multiplied the closer we got to the street overlooking the sea, where the police station was located. Maybe the idea of keeping Aunt Candace under control was a futile prospect, but I had to try, if just so we could get to the bottom of this before the murderer claimed another victim.

Edwin led the way into the building and asked his two troll guards to escort the pair of us through the door at the back which led to the holding cells. Aunt Candace ignored his instructions and marched straight through without a care in the world, coming to a halt in front of the cell which contained Betsy. A subdued-looking Haylee sat in the cell on her right.

"You did it," said Aunt Candace.

"Did what?" said Betsy. "I didn't kill Winona."

"Then how do you explain Tiffany dying after drinking the same wine that Winona gave her?" she said. "The whole bottle was poisoned. Don't deny it."

"She's dead?" said Haylee. "Tiffany?"

Aunt Candace gave her a glare, then turned her attention back onto Betsy. "Don't lie to me. Tiffany is dead, because someone poisoned her. The same someone who poisoned Winona, I don't doubt. Who could that be, I wonder?"

"It wasn't me," she said stubbornly. "You're accusing the wrong person. I wasn't even there."

"She drank the poisoned wine back when you were in the library, as you know well," said Aunt Candace. "You were jealous of her winning the prize from the start, and you made sure we all knew it."

"That's not..." She shrank backwards, her face pale. "I told you, I didn't do anything. I'm being set up."

"Are you now?" said Haylee from the neighbouring cell. "Sounds like a guilty conscience to me. I shouldn't be in here."

"When was the last time you spoke to Tiffany?" I asked Betsy.

She blinked. "Maybe an hour before the police took us away."

Haylee cleared her throat and looked me up and down. "Are you two even supposed to be in here?"

"What's it to you?" Aunt Candace retaliated. "Don't think I didn't see you trying to convince Tiffany to cowrite with you, as if she'd stoop that low."

Edwin cleared his throat from behind her. "That's enough, Candace. Do both of you deny having anything to do with Tiffany's death?"

"Of course," said Betsy in a tremulous voice. "I might have wanted to win the prize, but I wouldn't have killed anyone for it. Besides, I didn't even know Winona gave Tiffany that wine."

"Forgive me if I don't believe you," said Aunt Candace, but there was less heat in her voice than before. "Why else would both Tiffany and Winona have been the victims?"

"I didn't do it," Betsy insisted.

"And nor did I," Haylee said. "I want to speak to my lawyer."

"Be patient, Haylee," said Edwin. "I will speak to you later. You too, Betsy."

"If I had my way, you'd be here for the long haul." Aunt Candace's fervour had clearly gone, however, and she now looked as tired as I felt. She made no resistance as Edwin's trolls herded the pair of us out into the reception area.

"I will speak to them again," Edwin told her, "but I must ask you not to intervene. There is still the possibility that the killer remains in the library."

"Exactly," I said. "C'mon, Aunt Candace. We should head back and make sure Aunt Adelaide has got rid of that wine."

"Yes," said Aunt Candace. "I suppose it's up to us to make sure Betsy didn't hide any more poison inside the library."

To my relief, she turned away, and she and I walked out of the police station. I turned the corner and almost collided with Evangeline.

"Ack." I nearly jumped out of my skin. "Evangeline. What are you doing here?"

"I heard you were having some trouble at the library."

Aunt Candace gave her a bold stare. "Haven't got enough vampire drama to deal with, have you? Or did you and Edwin have an appointment?"

I suppressed the impulse to tell her to rein it in before she got herself bitten. Even if she did have a point. The leader of the town's vampires had nothing whatsoever to do with this case, though she had an annoying habit of inserting herself into my business even when it didn't involve her fellow vampires. Especially if she thought she might be able to gain something from it... like access to Laney or my dad's journal, for instance.

"No, I was curious, nothing more," said Evangeline.

"Right." I couldn't think why else she'd be interested. It wasn't like any of her fellow vampires were incarcerated here anymore, not now Mortimer Vale and his fellow Founders had been moved to a more secure facility outside the town.

"I assumed your friend might have offered to help with the investigation," said the vampire. "To speed up the process by reading the minds of the potential culprits."

Oh. *Oh.* Of course it was about Laney. "It's her choice to make, not mine."

"I suppose it is," she said. "I assume she's getting restless staying in the library. It's been long enough since she had contact with her fellow vampires that I have to worry about her development."

"She's getting on just fine," I said, refusing to be goaded. "She's in the library, after all, which has more guides to vampirism than anywhere else. And unlike you, it answers her questions."

"Is that so?" An amused smile exposed her fangs. "Perhaps you'll eventually see the error of your ways."

"As I said, it's Laney's choice, not mine," I told her.

"Then I suppose I will see you around, Aurora," she said.

She left on swift feet, while Aunt Candace and I remained outside the police station for a moment. It didn't seem like Edwin had noticed his visitor, and she hadn't shown herself to anyone except for me. She also hadn't seemed that interested in the prisoners at all.

Which meant the chances were high that she'd been waiting for us. I'd been dead right in my assumption that she was simply biding her time before she swooped in and tried to recruit Laney to her side. Or was she more interested in the journal, and had hoped to get a glimpse of its contents from my thoughts? There was no way to tell, but it was hard to shake the sinking feeling that the leader of the vampires had a point.

Perhaps mind-reading was the only remaining route to the answers.

10

Aunt Candace and I returned to the library to find the guests still isolated in the classroom at the back with two troll guards standing outside the door to prevent anyone from getting out. Aunt Adelaide and Estelle, meanwhile, stood in the Reading Corner nearby.

"We won't have anyone going missing again," Estelle was saying to her mother. "Nobody leaves without supervision. I have Spark watching everyone in the classroom and he'll alert me if anyone makes trouble."

"How was the jail?" Aunt Adelaide spotted Aunt Candace and me approaching. "Did Betsy Blake have anything to say?"

"She denied everything," I said. "She claimed she didn't know Winona gave Tiffany the wine, too."

"A likely story," said Aunt Candace from behind me. "She was making it all up. I know she was."

"Edwin is going to question them all again," I added.

Unfortunately, the odds of getting rid of our unwanted

guests by the end of the weekend were dwindling with each passing second. Unless someone admitted guilt, we'd be forced to accept all the guests as potential suspects by default.

"Maybe I'll go back and hurry up the process," said Aunt Candace. "I bet if I work hard enough on her, Betsy will crack and confess."

"You'll do no such thing," Aunt Adelaide said sternly. "Poor Edwin has enough to deal with."

"He does," I said. "Besides, don't forget it's Haylee whose perfume showed up all over the crime scene. Also, I'm still lost on how the stolen manuscript fits into this. There's no reason for Betsy to have taken it."

Aunt Candace had no response to that.

Estelle frowned. "Is there a chance someone else took the manuscript? Not the killer?"

"Then why would it show up in the Forbidden Room as evidence?" I asked. "I know, it's weird. Betsy still fits the profile of the killer, but Haylee hasn't exactly acted innocent, either."

Aunt Candace took a step back. "I did find something on Haylee's dispute with Winona earlier. I'll go and get that."

She marched off in the direction of our living quarters, while I released a sigh of relief. "For a moment back there, I thought she'd end up spending the night in jail herself again. I think Edwin is glad she gave up and left without starting a fight."

"Sorry for making you deal with her alone," said Estelle.

"Honestly, it was probably best that we got it over with," I said. "From Betsy's reaction, she was shocked at

Tiffany's death. She might be good at acting, though. And she *did* really want to win the prize, so the fact that the winner was the second person to die is hard to ignore."

"It's up to Edwin to question the suspects further," said Aunt Adelaide. "Candace isn't thinking rationally at the moment. It's lucky she didn't pick a public fight."

"She wanted to," I said. "Instead, she nearly picked a fight with Evangeline of all people on the way back home."

"Evangeline?" Estelle echoed, her brow furrowing. "What in the world was she doing at the jail?"

"Checking up on the prisoners, apparently," I said. "Or poking her nose into our business."

"No surprise there," said Aunt Adelaide. "She's been quiet lately. I assumed she was avoiding us until the guests go home."

"That, and biding her time," I said. "Letting us drop our guard before coming after Laney, or the journal. Or both."

I'd hoped she'd stay away for as long as possible, but Evangeline had made no secret of the fact that she wanted to recruit Laney to join her fellow vampires and I knew that the instant I looked away, she'd make her move. It didn't help that she also wanted to know the contents of my dad's journal, and once I'd read it, I'd never be able to slip up and let a vampire into my thoughts again. Not if I wanted the vampires to leave me be—especially the Founders. My dad's past aside, that was one major reason I'd been putting off reading the whole journal even before the contest had upended everything.

Yet Evangeline's suggestion that Laney should read the suspects' minds to find the killer had wormed its way into my head despite my best efforts. If only there was a way to do that without pressuring Laney to use her powers openly and put herself in the crosshairs of the other vampires, that is—and that was just one thing which might potentially go wrong in the process. Laney had already killed two vampires in an attempt to protect me, and the Founders would be out for her blood if they knew what she'd done. Evangeline had all but promised to protect her from the potential backlash if Laney agreed to trust her, but *I* didn't trust the conniving vampire leader not to hand her over to the Founders herself, given the chance.

"She ought to have the sense not to come here," said Aunt Adelaide. "I suppose she would get curious about the situation, however, given the number of outsiders in town."

Footsteps sounded as Aunt Candace descended the stairs and walked out into the library once again.

"I couldn't find much," she said, "but I did get this."

Aunt Candace pulled out her phone and held up an article to show us. The text was small, so I had to squint to read it, but it concerned a small publisher called Sunny Day Press which had been accused of fraud by none other than Winona herself. The person in charge of the publisher, Rhonda Mallory, had protested up until the very end, but had eventually been forced to pay compensation to the wronged authors.

"What's this got to do with Haylee?" I asked.

"Read it," said Aunt Candace. "*Quite* the scandal, though it was all hushed up, as you might expect."

"Hold on a moment." I looked up from the screen. "What scandal?"

"Sunny Day Press came under fire a few years ago

when the owner was accused of not paying its authors," said Aunt Candace. "A committee investigating fraud committed by small presses exposed the whole thing. The publisher then put out a statement saying there was a misunderstanding and the payments then mysteriously showed up in the authors' bank accounts. It wasn't until much later that the name of the person actually running the publisher came out into the open, and even then, it's only known in certain circles."

"Rhonda Mallory is Haylee?" I guessed. "Is that what their argument was about?"

"Yes." A glint of triumph shone in her eyes as she withdrew the phone and scrolled down through the article with her thumb. "Rhonda Mallory is her old alter ego. She dropped that pen name afterwards."

"You're saying Haylee's the one who ran Sunny Day Press?" said Estelle. "I thought she was an author, not a publisher."

"She was both," said Aunt Candace. "She started out publishing her own books and then expanded into a small press—not using her real name, of course. However, she took out a loan and then never made back the costs, which ended in disaster for most of the authors involved."

"Wow," I said. "I can see why she wouldn't want that to go public. I take it Winona knew about it all?"

"Not only that, she was part of the initial committee that exposed her," said Aunt Candace. "It seems Haylee asked to join the committee for the Merry Mysteries award a few months ago and Winona turned her down, citing her old publisher as the main reason. Haylee didn't like that a bit."

"So that's why they argued," I surmised. "Was Tiffany involved at all?"

"She declined an offer from the same publisher a while ago," said Aunt Candace. "Both of us did, in fact."

I frowned. "Would that be a motive for murdering both of them?"

"I doubt it," she said. "It was two years ago. There'd be no reason to wait until now to strike."

Even so, Haylee certainly had a good reason to hold a grudge against Winona. And who knew, maybe against Tiffany, too. Her name hadn't cropped up in the article, but since Haylee herself had been operating under a pseudonym when she'd run the publisher, anyone from among our current guests might have been involved.

Aunt Adelaide pursed her lips. "I'd pass that information on to Edwin—*not* now, Candace. I'll call him myself when I have a spare moment. I suppose the police will find the same information in their research, if they haven't already."

"I hope so." Too bad I'd already used up my chance of getting answers from the Book of Questions. Though knowing my luck, we'd be stuck here long enough that I'd be able to use tomorrow's question as well. If I could think of a decent one, that is.

Aunt Candace scoffed. "Frankly, I'm still more inclined to blame Betsy. She's the obvious choice, and always has been."

"And you think *she* stole Winona's manuscript?" said Aunt Adelaide. "Nobody has owned up to taking it yet. Of course, it might not be connected to the murders, but that leaves the question of why the Forbidden Room thought it counted as a clue."

"Well, Tiffany's body showed up not long after," I allowed. "But it's entirely possible that the Forbidden Room was just messing with me."

"Why would the killer have even taken the manuscript?" said Estelle. "It's unfinished. Not to mention Winona probably had a backup copy or two, so it's not like it's the only copy of the manuscript in existence."

"Fair point." I gave a scan of the lower floor, which seemed oddly empty without the guests strewn around the Reading Corner. My gaze landed on Sylvester, who perched on the balcony, pretending to be asleep. Would he allow me another trip into the Forbidden Room if I asked? Even if I gave him a whole roomful of balloons to attack, that was unlikely. He took the Book of Questions' rules seriously. "I don't know if the missing manuscript is linked. I mean, Beverly has spent half the day trying to get her hands on people's books. And didn't you think Haylee and Tiffany were both trying to sneak a look at your own manuscript, Aunt Candace?"

Aunt Candace scowled. "Yes, because Tiffany was in a dry patch and Haylee is opportunistic. Winona's book, though... is anyone going to read it and check for potential clues?"

Aunt Adelaide gave her sister a stern look. "Don't you even think about it."

"Oh, come on, it's not like the police are going to read the whole thing," said Aunt Candace. "They're just keeping it as evidence. What a waste. For all they know, there are clues in the book itself."

I was starting to wish I hadn't brought it up in front of Aunt Candace at all, but on the other hand, maybe it would give her something to do which didn't involve badgering the police and tormenting Edwin.

"Perhaps," said Aunt Adelaide. "If you're going to read the manuscript, don't leave it lying around unattended, Candace."

"What do you take me for?" she said. "I'll take good care of it."

I hope so. Because according to the Forbidden Room, it *was* evidence that pointed towards the killer, even if none of us could figure out how it was connected. Regardless, it was easier to let her have her own way. If the manuscript also turned up a clue or two about the killer by the time she got to the end, so much the better.

While Aunt Candace went to fetch the manuscript, Estelle, Aunt Adelaide and I were left to hold the fort downstairs in the library. Cass had yet to reappear, while the guests remained under supervision in the other classroom. At least tomorrow was Sunday, so we didn't have to worry about getting the place ready to reopen in the morning, but despite a thorough search of the ground floor, we had yet to find any traces of how the poison had been slipped into the wine. It must have been in someone's possession beforehand, unless the wine had been poisoned before anyone had even reached the library, but how could we be sure?

"Wish I'd found the rest of the poison in the Forbidden Room," I remarked to Estelle. "Then at least we'd know for certain it couldn't be used to poison anyone else."

"True," she said. "I might go into the Room myself and ask where it is, on the off-chance that there's a half-empty bottle of poison hidden somewhere in the library."

"Would that work, do you think?" I asked Aunt Adelaide.

"Only if the evidence is actually in the library," she said. "The killer might have disposed of it after the first or second murder. If the container is empty, it might not respond to the Room's magic, either."

That figured. "Do any of the guests know the Forbidden Room is a thing?"

"No," said Aunt Adelaide, "but they know the library is magical, and might have kept that in mind when they planned these murders."

"Wish I'd just asked the Book of Questions for the poison instead," I said. "Before Tiffany's death. Granted, they might've already slipped it into the wine bottle, but whatever container it was originally in can't have vanished into thin air."

"I'll ask the Room myself," said Aunt Adelaide. "Once I've finished setting up the security spells on the guest rooms."

"You're not letting everyone stay overnight again?" I said disbelievingly.

"Not the ones who are currently in custody," she said, "but the rest will have to stay here in the library. There's nobody else in town willing to take them in."

"Cass would tell you to make them camp in a field or something," I said. "What if the killer *is* among the people who are left in the library? I'm not saying there's an easy solution, but I don't blame the others for not feeling safe in here."

"It's not ideal, but it's the only option we have," said Aunt Adelaide. "Besides, the library is the ideal place to keep the culprit secure, if it comes down to it. We have enough magic in here to restrain them and the spells preventing anyone from leaving the library using magic are still in effect."

"They can still terrorise the others, though," I added. "Remember the wraith?"

Estelle winced. "Yes... I think I need to speak to Cass and let her know the guests will be staying another night."

"Want me to talk to her?" I asked.

"You already dealt with Aunt Candace," she said. "Take the evening off, Rory. Have a date with Xavier."

"I'm not leaving you here alone," I protested. "Besides, I should let Laney know they're staying, too."

"I'll speak to Cass, then," said Estelle. "Wish me luck."

"Good luck."

As she walked away, I went looking for Laney. I found her sitting on the sofa in the living quarters, looking more awake than she had before. Then again, it was growing dark, and the night was generally when she felt most alert. She'd left the lights off, though her skin held a faint glow which hadn't existed when she'd been human.

"Hey," I said to her. "You should know... the guests are staying another night."

To my surprise, she barely blinked. "I thought so. There wasn't much chance of getting the case wrapped up by the day's end. Some of them were staying the full weekend anyway."

"True," I said. "I think the killer is more likely to be among the people in custody than the ones here in the library. Betsy fits all the criteria except for stealing Winona's manuscript."

She tilted her head. "Speaking of which, what happened earlier with that book, anyway?"

"What book?"

"You know," she said. "You disappeared, then showed up out of nowhere with Winona's manuscript. Or to be more precise, you fell headfirst out of thin air and crash-landed in the Reading Corner."

Oh. I'd known she'd end up witnessing the Forbidden Room's magic eventually, and now was a good enough time to give her an explanation.

"There's a book called the Book of Questions which contains answers to any question you want to ask," I explained. "It's like the library's index, basically, but it has its own set of weird rules and each of us only gets to ask one question per day. When you open the book, you're transported inside it. Then you ask your question and if the Book feels like answering, it'll do so. Generally in a roundabout way."

"Wow," she said. "So… it's just for your family?"

"You've got it," I said. "I asked the room to give me some evidence which pointed to the killer and it threw the manuscript at me with no explanation before tossing me out into the Reading Corner."

"Oh," said Laney. "So that's how you knew the missing manuscript was linked to the killer?"

"Yes, but the Room didn't give me any more details," I said. "I can go back in there tomorrow and ask something else, since it looks like we have another day of questioning ahead of us, but I'd need to think of a better question this time."

Laney's gaze had turned intent, more so than it'd been before. In fact, her stillness brought a reminder of Evangeline's habit of watching my every movement, and it hit me that her mention of my appearance in the Reading

Corner had been a little too specific for someone who hadn't actually witnessed it. Had she read it from my thoughts?

Laney's expression shifted to guilt when I turned in her direction. "Sorry," she said. "It was an accident, but I slipped into your mind for a second there."

"You did?" What else had she seen? There was nothing in my mind that I wouldn't have shared with her anyway, but a fair few things I didn't want other people to know, and even more that I didn't want to share with the town's other mind-readers. Especially Evangeline.

"Sorry," Laney said again. "I didn't realise it'd be that easy. I mean, I've been struggling for ages to get a clear picture on someone's thoughts. I figured it'd be easier if I was alone with one person, like you said, but I didn't expect it to happen when I wasn't even trying."

"Don't worry about it," I said. "If anything, it's a sign that you're beginning to be able to get some control over it. You've been trying for ages, right?"

"I have," she said. "And... I think I'd like to try mind-reading on the guests."

"You do?" Surprise laced my tone.

"Yeah," she said. "You were right... it's probably the only way to get any honesty out of anyone here. I'd have to speak to each of them alone, but I reckon I can narrow it down if I do it that way. I've been practising."

My mouth pressed together. "I'd have to go with you if I wanted to do the questioning, but I won't distract you, will I?"

"Nah, you're less distracting than anyone else," she said. "Especially if I concentrate on the person whose mind I'm reading. Is that okay?"

"Sure," I said. "We need to figure out how to do this without the guests actually realising you're reading their thoughts, though. Some of them might have training to resist vampire mind-reading, for all I know, and if they realise what you are, they might kick up a fuss."

Even in the magical world, not everyone had the skill to resist a vampire. I'd only needed to learn because of my propensity for running into vampire-related trouble, but it was possible to only encounter the undead in passing or to not register them as a threat. I wouldn't lie, that sounded like a simpler existence. Laney's condition had helped me become a little more comfortable with being around the undead, but I wished the mind-reading issue was easier for me to handle.

"Ah," she said. "Never thought of that. Is it common, then?"

"Hard for me to judge," I admitted. "Since vampires were the first paranormals I met."

"No wonder you had to learn fast," she said. "I don't want to cause you any more stress, Rory. I know how you have good reason to hate the vampires."

"I don't hate them," I said. "I could never hate *you*. You're nothing like the Founders. Or Evangeline either. Besides, helping you learn how to use your vampire abilities has helped *me* get used to being around vampires. It's good for both of us."

A smile came to her mouth. "You sure?"

"Of course." If she read my thoughts, she'd know I meant it. "If you really want to give it a try, let's go and read some minds."

11

First, Laney and I went looking for Estelle and found her near the front desk in the lobby.

"How was Cass?" I asked. "Did she blow up at you?"

"She grunted at me and didn't come out of the corridor upstairs," Estelle responded.

"Sounds about right," I said. "Laney and I had an idea."

"Oh?" Her gaze flickered between the two of us, curiosity in her eyes.

"We're wondering if we can speak to some of the guests individually," I said. "Laney wants to give mind-reading a try to see if we can turn up some new information."

"She does?" she said. "Anyone in particular?"

"I'll see what I can pick up from everyone's surface thoughts first," Laney said. "That might help me narrow it down."

"All right." Estelle led the way across to the classroom

where the guests had been sequestered and spoke to the troll guarding the door.

My pulse thrummed with nervousness as we waited, though it was Laney who had the most to risk. She was also the least afraid of the pair of us, which wasn't anything new. Laney had been fearless *before* her transformation into a vampire, and now I worried a little about her newfound semi-invincible state making her more reckless than usual. On the other hand, I didn't see a better way to get to the truth than via a direct link to the minds of the suspects. Evangeline didn't have to know anything at all.

The troll stepped aside, allowing Estelle to open the door. As soon as she walked into the classroom, Beverly sprang over.

"Oh, hello," she said. "I thought you'd come with an update. Have you spoken to the police?"

Several others crowded in behind her. I spotted Alana in the background, scribbling in a notebook, but the others were more interested in seeing if we were going to let them out. Laney went stock-still, her gaze fixed on Beverly, and Estelle stepped in to rescue us. "We're not letting everyone out of the room yet. Can you move away from the door?"

As she moved to herd the guests backwards before someone managed to sneak out, I inched closer to Laney. "Are you okay?"

Laney turned to me. "*She* stole the manuscript."

"What?" I stared at her. "Who?"

"Beverly." She dropped her voice. "I think she wanted to read it. It's hard to get a handle on her thoughts, to tell you the truth, but she's definitely the person who took it."

Beverly? It wasn't that implausible, given her endless attempts to get her hands on the other authors' manuscripts, but did that make her connected to the killer? According to the Forbidden Room, it did, yet I had trouble seeing the excitable teen girl as being capable of poisoning two of her idols. It didn't add up at all.

"And... the murderer?" I whispered. "Any clues there?"

"No." She shook her head. "I need to get closer."

I glanced over at Beverly, who was currently begging Estelle to let everyone out of the classroom again. "I'll ask if she can talk to us alone."

Estelle heard the end of my sentence and shuffled back out of the room. "Who do you want to talk to?"

"Beverly."

Hearing her name, Beverly's head snapped in our direction. "Yes?"

I beckoned to her. "Can I have a word with you? Alone?"

"Of course." She bounded out of the room into the Reading Corner and sat down on a nearby bean bag, almost toppling off it in surprise when Laney approached soundlessly from nearby. "Are you one of the authors, too?"

"No, I'm Rory's friend," said Laney.

"You're a vampire," she said. "Oh, did you inspire one of Candace's books? Where is she right now, anyway?"

"She's working on her manuscript," I told her.

Her eyes flared with interest. "Really? Is she going to give us a preview?"

"Probably not." I sidestepped into the right line of questioning. "Winona's manuscript going missing has made her reluctant to share anything."

"Oh." Her face fell, her fingers fiddling with the hem of her shirt, and I didn't need to be able to read her mind to see the guilt in her expression.

"Did you take the manuscript?" I asked. "I'm not accusing you of doing anything to Winona, but if we know who took her manuscript, it'll make it much easier to figure out if it's relevant or not. I won't tell Edwin or the others it was you."

Not if she wasn't the killer, anyway. Though the question remained of why the Forbidden Room had designated the manuscript as evidence connected to the murders. Perhaps Beverly might be able to point me in the right direction.

Her shoulders hunched. "I just wanted to read it, but when Winona died, I panicked and hid it over there in the stacks."

"Whereabouts?" I asked.

She frowned. "I thought you found it."

"I used a spell to bring it directly to me," I said, which was pretty much true. "The spell didn't point me to where it was hidden. Where did you put it?"

"Just there." She pointed towards the front of the library. "In the research section, behind a huge book with a red cover."

"Okay," I said. "Thanks for telling me."

"You won't tell everyone, will you?" she said tremulously. "The others will never let me come to their events again if they find out."

"Of course I won't," I said. "You don't know anything about who poisoned Winona, do you?"

"No."

I glanced at Laney, but I couldn't discern whether

she'd read anything from Beverly's mind from her expression. "All right. You'd better go back into the classroom."

I caught Estelle's eye, and she walked over to escort Beverly over to join the other guests again. Meanwhile, Laney and I headed into the stacks. When we were out of view of the classroom, she raised an eyebrow at me. "I didn't get anything useful from her. Her thoughts are all over the place. She hid the manuscript somewhere in here?"

"It's worth looking to see if anything else was hidden in the same place." I headed deeper into the stacks, towards the research section of the library. "In case that was the real clue. The Forbidden Room isn't known for giving me direct answers."

"Wow," she remarked. "That sounds like a challenge to deal with."

"You've no idea." I walked on, Laney easily overtaking me with swift vampire steps, until we reached the area immediately behind the front desk. From there, I scanned the area for anything out of place and spotted an empty section of shelf where a large red book had been moved to the side. "Can you smell anything strange over here?"

"That perfume again." She sniffed the bookshelves. "Definitely the same. It's practically clinging to the shelves."

"Damn." Did that mean Haylee had been in here, too? Or had she touched the manuscript before Beverly had got her hands on it? Perhaps she'd just walked through while exploring the library yesterday, instead, but her perfume had certainly ended up in some odd places.

"It's a strong scent," she said. "Strong enough to cover

anything else, but it might not be deliberate. Unless they knew I was a vampire."

"They don't, and let's hope it stays that way." Beverly had figured it out, though, but it was hard to hide the natural speed and grace of the undead. My heart gave an uneasy flip as I recalled Evangeline and her mysterious appearance at the jail, plus my growing suspicion that she wouldn't wait for much longer before trying to make a claim on Laney. Especially if she learned about her improved mind-reading abilities as well as her involvement in the investigation. "I didn't think of the possibility of the scent being used to cover up something else, though."

Had the killer left the perfume everywhere on purpose? If Beverly was innocent of the murder, that still left a fair few people to question, but I wasn't sure Laney's mind-reading stamina would hold up for that long. Especially with everyone currently arguing with Estelle about being stuck in the classroom, and two of our major culprits in police custody. Including Haylee herself.

"Want me to speak to someone else next?" asked Laney.

"Better wait for Aunt Adelaide to return from the Forbidden Room, I think," I replied. "I need to tell her about the perfume."

"Okay, sure," she said. "I... um, need to raid the blood supplies."

"Go ahead." I waved her off, as if it was no big deal. Which it wasn't, not really. Not as much as the notion of her reading my thoughts, at any rate, which was more due to my worry that my hidden thoughts would make it back to Evangeline—or worse, the Founders. If Laney accidentally slipped into my thoughts while I was reading my dad's journal, for instance, any of the other vampires might be able to pick that information out of her head. She was no longer drinking the potion which blocked mind-reading, and even if she learned to shield her thoughts the way I had, she'd still be susceptible to the more powerful vampires delving into her mind.

Which left a massive question mark over whether I should risk reading the entirety of my dad's journal at all as long as Laney lived here in the library. If we weren't careful, the situation might evolve into a perfect storm of the vampire variety which would make the murders the least of our problems.

I reached the front of the library and found Aunt Adelaide putting the Book of Questions away. "Any luck?"

"No," she said. "I asked the book to show me where the bottle of poison the killer put in the wine was hidden, and it threw a basic book of poisons at me instead. If I didn't know better, the Room was reprimanding me for asking."

"Wouldn't surprise me," I said. "I have some news, though. Laney and I found out Beverly is the one who stole Winona's unfinished manuscript. Turns out she hid it downstairs in the research section."

Her brows rose. "She confessed?"

"After Laney read her mind." I explained our conversation with Beverly and what we'd learned from her.

"She just wanted to read the book, nothing more," concluded Aunt Adelaide.

"Laney said she couldn't read any thoughts which pointed to her being the killer," I added. "Unless she managed to keep Laney away from those thoughts, of course, but she doesn't strike me as the type to be wily enough to conceal her thoughts from vampires."

"Is Laney going to read the minds of the other suspects?" she asked.

"Not the ones in police custody, and the others are getting restless in the classroom," I said. "Also, I'm not sure it's a good idea to let her condition go public, given Evangeline's comments earlier."

"You spoke to Evangeline?" asked Aunt Adelaide. "Where?"

"She was hanging around the police station pretending she wasn't nosing around for information on the murders," I explained. "I'd rather avoid drawing her attention again if I can help it. I know Laney isn't afraid of her, but I feel like she was waiting for the opportunity to speak to me about her."

I didn't doubt Laney's confidence, but Evangeline was centuries old and had no moral scruples whatsoever. Her desire for knowledge and control over all other vampires had no bounds, and I'd never completely dismissed my suspicion of her involvement with the Founders.

"I don't doubt she is," said Aunt Adelaide. "I never checked with Laney about how she's getting on with her vampire training, though. I didn't know she could do one-on-one mind-reading without side effects."

"She's working on it," I said. "She also did a scan of everyone in the classroom and figured out Beverly took the manuscript, so she's getting better at dipping into people's thoughts without getting overwhelmed."

I didn't want to tell her that she'd done the same to me, though, because then I'd have to admit to my own mixed feelings about her newly honed abilities. I didn't want

Laney to think I was afraid of her, because I wasn't. I'd get past my unease in time, and it wasn't worth causing damage to our friendship in the short-term while I tried to adjust to the idea of her being able to peek at my inmost thoughts.

"Well, good on her," said Aunt Adelaide. "Where was the manuscript, then?"

"Over there." I pointed to the right shelves. "We went looking around the area for more clues, but all we found was that perfume scent again."

"Haylee's perfume?" she said.

"The same one, yeah." I wished Laney could question her—and Betsy, too, while she was at it—but I doubted Edwin would consent to letting a vampire interrogate his suspects, and besides, Evangeline had been waiting there for a reason.

Laney herself reappeared a moment later, and I hastily blanked my thoughts.

"There you are," said Aunt Adelaide. "It sounds like you've been practising your skills a lot. I'm impressed you managed to see into Beverly's thoughts without any others intervening."

"Her mind was all over the place, so it was hard to pin anything down," said Laney. "But I don't think she's the killer."

"Did you get anything from the others that's worth looking into?" I asked.

She shook her head. "No, but I only gave them a brief scan. I might've missed something."

Unless the killer wasn't here, and they were among the group of major suspects already locked in the holding cells. Like the person whose perfume kept showing up—

and who'd been involved in fraud years ago which might have impacted anyone here.

"Who do you want me to question next?" she asked.

"Maybe we should leave it until tomorrow," I said. "I mean, the people in police custody are the top of the suspect list, so they're more likely to have useful information in their thoughts. But you'd have to ask Edwin's permission to speak to them, and he's still doing the questioning himself."

"Oh." Her brow furrowed. "Makes sense."

It was pretty obvious we needed more evidence before we could throw out any more accusations, besides. While I could ask the Forbidden Room another question after midnight, I'd need to plan better if I was to get the information I needed rather than hitting yet another dead end.

"At this rate, it'll have to wait until the morning," I added. "What's the plan for the night? We're not leaving everyone locked up in the classroom, are we?"

"No, we'll move them back to their guest rooms and order catering to be sent upstairs," Aunt Adelaide said. "Sylvester is going to watch to make sure nobody tries to poison anything."

"I'm sure he'll be thrilled at that," I commented. "Is Cass staying upstairs with the animals for the long haul?"

"Probably," said Aunt Adelaide. "I'd offer to take her some food, but she probably conjured up her own. She's self-sufficient enough to hole up there for weeks at a time if she wants to avoid us."

"This better not last for weeks," I said. "I mean, we're meant to reopen the library to the public on Monday."

"Yes, and I'd rather we deal with this situation before then," said Aunt Adelaide, echoing my thoughts. "We all know there are certain individuals who'd be all too happy to take advantage of our closure to dampen our reputation. Estelle knows it, too."

I'd bet she did. I felt bad for her, seeing another event derailed by murder, but I couldn't think of anything more I could do to solve the case, short of taking Laney with me to the jail to question the prisoners. If Edwin agreed to it, that is.

We usually ate dinner together as a family, but when I went to knock on Aunt Candace's door, she refused to come out of her research cave.

"I've just reached an important part in Winona's book," she said from behind the closed door.

"What's it even about?" I asked.

"It's a murder mystery about a woman who fed her husband to a bunch of alligators," Aunt Candace replied. "Now, go away and stop bothering me."

"Aren't you interested to hear that Beverly was the one who stole the manuscript?" I said.

"Was she, now?" She shuffled over and opened the door a crack to peer at me. "Not a total surprise, I admit. I always thought the killer and the thief weren't the same person."

"Yeah, but the confusing thing is that there was the scent of Haylee's perfume all over the place where it was hidden," I said.

"Which proves nothing," she said. "She's been all over the ground floor, I don't doubt. I still think Betsy's the murderer. She has the most obvious motive."

"I don't disagree," I said. "I just wish I knew why the Forbidden Room thought that manuscript counted as evidence when Beverly was the one who stole it and she's not the murderer."

Quite possibly, Sylvester had been messing with me all along, telling me to use my own skills to figure out the identity of the culprit. Who even knew.

"I have absolutely no idea." The door closed again. "I'll let you know when I get to the end."

I left Aunt Candace to read the manuscript and went to join the rest of my family downstairs. After a quiet dinner, I went upstairs for an early night. My dad's journal called to me, awakened by Evangeline's taunts, and while part of me remained wary of Laney reading my thoughts, curiosity won out.

After I'd settled on the bed, I opened to the most recent page and began to read my dad's thoughts from years ago, when I was a small child.

I'm beginning to think the vampires are avoiding me on purpose. They're certainly elusive, I'll give them that. I suppose their natural instincts for spectacle will eventually win out and they'll throw a large gathering. Then I'll be able to corner them.

I looked up from the page, my thoughts spinning. What did he mean? Had he been *looking* for the vampires? I'd assumed they were hunting him, not the other way around.

"Partner," squeaked a voice.

I dropped the journal, which slid off the bed onto the floor. "Jet, don't sneak up on me in the dark like that."

"But it's important!" The crow flitted onto the bed. "Your friend is outside the library."

"What?" I climbed off the bed and retrieved the book. "You mean Laney?"

"Yes," he said. "She went out. I thought you'd want to know."

Oh, no. I grabbed my cloak and shoes and shoved them on, then headed out of my room and ran downstairs. The library was silent, its towering shelves lit by the floating lanterns which appeared each night, but I didn't stop to appreciate the view. When I opened the front door, I spotted Laney's lithe silhouette disappearing from sight across the town square, faster than any regular human was capable of.

She wasn't on her way to sneak into the jail and speak to the suspects, was she? Maybe she'd picked up on my thoughts earlier after all, but she hadn't been out in the open since before she'd been bitten, and other vampires roamed the town at night.

I had to get her back to the library before Evangeline reached her first.

12

I walked after Laney as fast as I possibly could, but she moved like a living shadow through the night, so fast she might as well have been a mirage. She flitted down the side street alongside the clock tower, and my heart sank when she rounded the corner towards the police station.

Why hadn't it occurred to me that her restlessness was reaching its peak and she was bound to give into her instincts to go out at night eventually? For all I knew, she was stealthy enough to get away with sneaking into the jail to speak to the prisoners without alerting the guards, but she'd have to face some serious questions if she got caught in there. Then there was no chance Evangeline wouldn't find out and get involved.

I swore under my breath when she disappeared into the police station. I'd missed my chance to catch her, and even using a spell to hide myself ran the risk of alerting the police's attention. I possessed none of a vampire's stealth or grace, so I'd be more of a hindrance than a help if I went after her now.

Several seconds passed as I hovered outside the police station, shrinking back against the wall to hide myself from view. A cold breeze blew off the sea, making me shiver. And then without warning, Evangeline appeared at my side, a wide smile on her pretty face. My heart leapt into my throat.

"Fancy seeing you here again, Aurora Hawthorn," the vampire said softly.

"Evangeline." I buried my freezing hands inside my cloak pockets, now shivering for reasons entirely unrelated to the cold. "What are you doing here?"

"I saw your friend," she said. "It looks like she's roaming around of her own accord now, isn't she?"

My hands clenched. "She's free to do as she likes. She doesn't need to consult you before leaving the library."

"I don't disagree," she said mildly. "It's Edwin's permission she needs to ask if she wants to question his prisoners in the dead of night without supervision."

Damn. Unfortunately, she was right, but if I went in there myself, I was more likely to draw the guards' attention than Laney was. Which Evangeline herself knew perfectly well. It wouldn't surprise me if she wanted to goad me into drawing attention to both of us, and I refused to rise to the bait.

"Yes, I know," I hissed. "You need to leave. You're not supposed to be here either."

"I'm not trespassing, unlike your friend," she said. "If Laney succeeds in tracking the killer, that indicates her mind-reading skills are sufficient enough that she is more than ready to be educated by another vampire in order to make the most of her considerable talents."

"That's up to her, not you," I responded.

A fanged smile curled her lip. "You can't keep her from being around her own kind, Aurora. I told you so, more than once, but you still refuse to see the truth in front of your own face."

I managed to hold her gaze by sheer willpower. "She isn't like you."

She laughed. "You think all vampires are the same as I am? Do you believe all humans are identical, too?"

"Laney was a normal before she turned," I countered. "That's completely different to growing up in the magical world. She's also younger than most of you and has no ties here in Ivory Beach aside from with me and my family. The library is her best shot of learning all about being a vampire before—"

"Before what?" she said. "Before she goes home to the normal world and returns to that mundane customer service job of hers?"

"You—" I broke off. Inside me, anger warred with the instincts telling me I shouldn't be antagonising her, but she had no right to dictate my best friend's choices. "It's none of your business whatsoever. She already told me she has no intention of joining your team even if she does decide to live here in Ivory Beach. She chose to stay with us in the library instead."

"You have yet to allow me the chance to speak to her about what living with my fellow vampires would entail," she said. "If she hasn't been presented with all the options, how can she be expected to make up her mind?"

"She knows exactly what joining you means." And so

did I. Manipulation, cruelty, inhumanity, and a lot more besides.

"I think not, Aurora," she said. "I would prefer not to make an enemy of either of you, but you are lying to yourself when you claim that your friend's loyalty towards you is absolute. She isn't the same person you knew before she became one of us."

"Someone else claimed to know Laney better than I do," I said. "Mortimer Vale. It didn't end well for him."

Her smile made the hairs stand up on my arms, and for an instant, I wondered if I'd have to use the firedust I kept in my bag to warn her off after all.

"No," she said, "it didn't. I suspect that he and his friends little expected to get themselves into such a conundrum when they went after your father's journal, but with them out of the way, there's nothing to stop you from getting the information you need. Yet from what I've observed, you continue to delay making progress on reading the journal. One might even say you are stalling. Are you concerned your friend will pluck the answers from your mind?"

My heart sank to hear my fears confirmed. It seemed her goal of getting her hands on the journal itself had indeed shifted to reading that information from my thoughts instead. Or Laney's. Before I could respond, however, a yell rang out from inside the jail.

"Vampire!" yelled Betsy's voice, loud and clear.

A moment later, Laney sprinted through the doors in a blur, flying past Evangeline and me without even seeing us.

"Wait!" I hurried after her and caught her up alongside the clock tower. "Laney—stop!"

"Rory?" She skidded to a halt and spun around in a blur. "What are you doing?"

"Following you." I bent double, catching my breath. "Betsy saw you, didn't she? I heard her yelling."

"She was overreacting," said Laney. "She could tell I wasn't going to do her any harm from the other side of the cell door, but I startled her by mistake."

"Come on," I said. "We need to go back to the library. It's not safe out here."

"Rory, I'm not human, remember?" She strode forward confidently. "I'm fine. If anyone else woke up and alerted the police, they won't catch me."

"They might catch *me*," I pointed out. "They might also conclude you're the person who broke in, anyway, if Betsy gives an accurate description of you."

"Then you don't want to know what I read from her thoughts?" she said.

"Laney." I tried to keep my tone calm, but my heart was racing, and I was sure Evangeline was still hiding out of sight nearby. "Please."

"It wasn't her," said Laney. "She's not the killer. I saw into her thoughts, loud and clear."

I gaped at her, momentarily forgetting my panic. "Betsy isn't the killer at all? What about Haylee? And the others?"

"I didn't get close enough to read Haylee's thoughts before Betsy started screaming," she said. "I can go back in later."

"Not without permission," I insisted. "You must know how risky this is—"

We both stopped dead in our tracks as Evangeline

stepped out in front of us, her long curly hair blowing gently in the breeze off the seafront.

"Hello, Laney," Evangeline said in her soft, melodic voice.

"Evangeline," she responded. Her tone was neutral, almost bored, but the hairs on my arms stood on end as Evangeline turned her fanged smile on Laney.

I shot the vampires' leader a warning look which she entirely ignored. *Don't you even think about it,* I thought, as clearly as I could manage.

Evangeline didn't even acknowledge my pointed stare or the thoughts I projected at her, keeping her attention on Laney. "I hear you're adapting admirably to your transformation into a vampire."

"Who'd you hear that from?" she said.

"Oh, it's obvious from the way you're roaming the town at night," she said. "I have to say, it's a delight to see. I did wonder if hiding in the library, away from your fellow vampires, would stunt your progress, but it looks as though that hasn't been the case for you."

"Why are you complimenting me?" said Laney. "What do you want?"

My shoulders tensed again. Evangeline was as dangerous to her fellow vampires as she was to humans, and Laney was doubly vulnerable because of her connection to me. Her past as a normal and the consequent lack of the usual knowledge she'd have gained from growing up in the paranormal world made me feel protective of her despite knowing she was more than capable of handling herself.

"As leader of the town's vampires, it's my job to keep an eye on fledglings like you," Evangeline said in silky tones. "I can't have you going out of bounds and getting into trouble with the police, can I? It wouldn't look good for the rest of us if you were to get caught reading prisoners' minds when you hadn't been given permission to be in there."

"You don't have a clue what's been going on in the library in the last week," Laney said to her. "If you were in my position, you'd have done the same. Besides, I didn't know I had to ask your permission before going anywhere."

"I think you're misinformed on how connected I am to the activities taking place in this town," she said. "Don't believe everything you hear about me and about my fellow vampires. We take good care of each other and we look out for our own."

Laney made a sceptical noise. "I'm more under the impression you're only interested in me because you want to exploit me for your own convenience."

"Have you seen any evidence of that?" she enquired.

Laney didn't answer for a long moment. Admittedly, Evangeline took great care to pretend to be civil on the surface, but I hadn't actually told Laney about the mess with Dominic and the journal which had first given me the suspicion that she was more scheming than she let on. Maybe I should have, but there'd never been a good time, and I hadn't wanted to give Evangeline any more ammunition against my best friend.

"I know you're in charge of all the vampires in town," Laney finally said, "but Mortimer Vale is my... my sire, or whatever you call it. He's the one who created me, but that sure as hell doesn't mean *he* gets to decide what I do. So why should you get to do the same?"

"I am not Mortimer Vale," said Evangeline. "I will offer you a choice, but I would love to have the opportunity to explain to you the advantages of living with your fellow vampires, or at the very least taking lessons from us. No manipulation will be involved."

"Uh-huh," said Laney. "I won't take your word for it on that. I know you've been hassling Rory about that journal ever since you found out it existed."

Despite the dread gnawing at me, I silently cheered for Laney. She wouldn't give an inch, not even against the leader of the vampires. If only that would be enough to convince Evangeline to leave her alone.

"Whatever transpires between Aurora and myself will have no impact on whether I will welcome you to join my fellow vampires or not," she said. "It is my position to help out any of my kin in Ivory Beach, regardless of their circumstances, including yourself. I will be able to help you find the best way to use your considerable talents without human limitations."

"Do you normally offer to teach newbie vampires?" Laney asked.

"Yes," she said. "I do. You might not believe me, but there are so few of us compared to other paranormals, and we're a unique species with a number of talents which are woefully misunderstood by the magical world as a whole. Yes, even including your friends and family."

I didn't miss the way her gaze flickered in my direction as she spoke, as though insinuating that Laney couldn't trust me *or* my family to have her best interests at heart.

"I don't think vampires in general are misunderstood," said Laney. "I think living in a creepy old church and sneaking up on people might explain why other paranormals are wary around you in particular."

Go, Laney!

Evangeline's smile had long since disappeared, as though it'd sunk in that she was losing the argument. So she played her last hand.

"Does Aurora mind you reading her thoughts?" she asked Laney. "Because I'm not so sure she does. Certain members of her family definitely won't stand for it. In fact, I'm guessing you're having trouble getting Aurora's cousin, for once, to be civil to you, and that will only get worse with time."

Laney glanced at me. "What does that matter to you?"

"I can teach you how to control your abilities," she said. "I have many resources at my disposal and no ill intentions."

Laney was silent for a long moment. "You haven't said what the catch is."

"There isn't one," said Evangeline. "I'm inviting you to listen to what I have to say and to meet your fellow vampires. Then you can make your mind up. If you want to return to the library afterwards, you're welcome to do so, and I will do nothing to stop you."

"Laney," I began.

"Quiet, Aurora," said Evangeline. "Let her decide."

"All right," said Laney. "I'll come with you and hear you out."

Laney. "Evangeline, don't—"

"It's your friend's choice," Evangeline interrupted. "I'll thank you to let her make the decision for herself.

My hands clenched and my eyes burned. "If you hurt

her, then my entire family will come after you. I can promise you that."

She made no reply. When Laney took a hesitant step over to her side, she turned around and walked away. Laney shot me an apologetic look, but she continued to follow the leading vampire

until both of them had vanished from sight.

Laney was gone. And I couldn't shake the feeling that it was my fault.

13

I returned to the library, wrapped in a dark cloud of despair. When I entered, I thought there was nobody in the reception area, but then a pair of bright yellow eyes blinked at me from the shadows and made me jump. "Really, Sylvester. You didn't need to scare me like that."

"What's up with you?" said the owl. "You look like someone kicked you. Where's that friend of yours?"

My eyes stung with tears. "Gone. She went with Evangeline to stay with the vampires for a bit."

I didn't particularly want to talk about her choice with Sylvester, who was second only to Cass in his dislike of Laney and had made no secret of his disapproval of her staying in the library over the last few weeks.

"Oh," said the owl. "Interesting. I have to admit, I didn't think she'd say yes."

I blinked. "You didn't? I thought you didn't want her to stay."

"That's not the same as expecting her to choose the library over the vampires," he said. "I assumed she was wise to Evangeline's trickery."

"She is," I said. "But she decided to go and hear her out anyway. Evangeline pretended she had no agenda and told Laney that she'll get to meet her fellow vampires and have lessons from them. I hoped she'd say no, but she just... went."

"Then she might come back if she doesn't like what she hears," said Sylvester. "What was she even doing outside the library? Will nobody in here do as they're told?"

"She went to the jail to read the other suspects' minds," I said. "Yes, I know it was a bad idea for her to go alone, but she was impatient, like the rest of us, so she decided to go and get answers for herself."

"It wasn't a bad idea," he said.

"I'm sorry, what?" I blinked at him again. "Are you saying she had a point?"

"I wouldn't go that far," he said, "but it's true that she made a decision which made sense to her, given her newfound talents. Did Edwin catch her at it?"

"Nope, Betsy did," I said. "She screamed her head off when she realised there was a vampire inside the jail. Laney did read her mind first and told me she wasn't the culprit, but now we're back at square one."

This time, without my best friend to help us.

"Your friend should have spoken to someone else," said Sylvester. "Betsy was the obvious choice... too obvious in my opinion."

"Do you have any theories, then?" I asked. "Haylee's

perfume was all over the crime scene, but I thought she was too obvious a choice as well. Not to mention I don't know if she and Tiffany really knew each other well at all. But if it's not Betsy, then who is it? Did Beverly somehow manage to hide her thoughts about the murder from Laney when she read her mind?"

"I wouldn't know," said Sylvester. "I can't read minds. I'm an owl."

"You have all the knowledge of the library," I pointed out. "Do you really have no other evidence to give to me?"

"I think you've already done enough searching for physical evidence," the owl responded. "You need to think outside of the box."

"Was that a reference to the Forbidden Room?" I said. "Because Aunt Adelaide wasn't impressed with what she found in there either. Is it worth waiting until after midnight to ask another question?"

"Not if you do the same as last time," he said. "Your questions are so pedestrian."

"Hey, I can only work with what I have," I said. "It's not like anyone's confessed so far. None of the guests are causing trouble, are they?"

"Everyone is on their best behaviour, including me," he said.

"Uh-huh." Behind the owl, I could hear footsteps inside the living quarters, and I knew I had to break the news about Laney's departure to my family. "Okay. I'm heading off. Maybe I can come up with a new theory overnight."

Not that I felt like sleeping. My mind spun in circles after what Sylvester had said, while pangs of guilt at

Laney's choice kept nagging at me. Luckily, I found Estelle in the kitchen, making hot chocolate.

"Hey, Rory," she said. "Want some of this?"

"Please." I walked over to her. "It finally happened. Evangeline got to Laney."

"How?" asked Estelle. "She didn't go out, did she?"

"She went to the police station," I said. "To read the prisoners' minds."

Estelle groaned quietly. "I know she's a vampire and she's stealthier than the rest of us, but I assumed she wouldn't take the risk. I should've known better."

"She got impatient," I said. "Wanted to talk to the suspects. I think it's my fault for putting the idea into her head."

"Did she get anywhere with the prisoners, then?" she asked.

"She found out Betsy Blake isn't the killer," I said. "But Betsy saw her and raised the alarm. On top of that, Evangeline ambushed her outside and talked her into going with her to join the other vampires, and now I'm not sure she'll come back."

"Oh, Rory." Estelle wrapped me in a hug. "She hasn't ditched you. She's probably just curious about the other vampires. She hasn't been outside the library for weeks."

"True, but now really isn't the best time," I said. "Also, Evangeline basically accused us of portraying her as an evil manipulator and said that she could prove to Laney that she's a nice person after all. I think she's been waiting for the chance to try indoctrinating Laney for a while, but I never expected it to work."

Estelle handed me my mug of hot chocolate and we walked into the living room.

"She's definitely crafty," said Estelle. "How'd she manage to sway Laney into going with her, then? What did she promise?"

"She said she'd introduce her to all the other vampires." I sat down and sipped at my drink, the delicious warmth soothing my nerves a little. "She also promised she'd teach her to control her mind-reading powers, and she got in a dig against me while she was at it, because Laney read my mind earlier and it freaked me out a little."

"Oh," she said. "She wasn't in control, right?"

"She said it was an accident," I said. "And I believed her, but I'm worried Evangeline will take advantage of our friendship to read things about me from Laney's mind. I know it's selfish, but…"

"It isn't," she said. "You have a good reason to worry about Evangeline peeking into your thoughts."

"Especially now I'm reading my dad's journal," I added. "If Laney reads anything about the journal from my thoughts, Evangeline all but told me she'll be ready and waiting to read her mind. She pretty much admitted outright that the reason she gave up on the idea of getting her hands on the journal is because now she has Laney instead."

"Ugh." Estelle pulled a face. "I think Laney is strong, though. Maybe she wants to learn to control her mind-reading talents precisely so that she can stop Evangeline from taking advantage."

"I guess she might be," I relented. "But she also seemed interested in meeting the other vampires as well."

"Then might she have wanted to do some spying of her own?" Estelle suggested. "She must be curious about the others, and she hasn't met any vampires except for Evangeline."

"And Mortimer Vale and his friends," I added. "I know, maybe she's just curious. She can take care of herself, but Evangeline... it's obvious she has another agenda here."

"I'm sure she does," said Estelle. "I think you can trust Laney to make the right choice, though."

Did I? I trusted her as a friend, without question, but she was known for being impulsive and that trait hadn't been dampened by her transformation into a vampire. Look at how she'd killed those vampires who'd threatened my life... not to mention her recent choice to break into the jail under cover of night to read the prisoners' minds. On the flip side of that, I had little doubt that if she suspected the other vampires had a less than stellar opinion of me or were plotting against my family, she'd be out of there in a heartbeat.

Yes, I trusted her. But the fact remained that we might well have lost our shot at reading the minds of the other potential suspects, and if Evangeline got her claws in Laney, it'd be that much harder for her to escape.

"I guess." I took another sip of my hot chocolate. "This is not good timing. On top of Betsy turning out to be innocent, I mean."

If word got out about a vampire being seen sneaking around the jail, it might make it harder to get the truth from the real culprit, too. Beverly seemingly hadn't suspected Laney of reading her thoughts, but she wasn't the murderer either. All our attempts to get answers had led us into dead ends.

Estelle and I sat and drank our hot chocolate in companionable silence for a few minutes before she spoke again. "Betsy has an obvious motive, true, but losing the prize is only one possible reason to commit murder. She doesn't have a personal connection to the victims."

"And Haylee does?" I dug out my phone and found my internet connection was working for once, so I ran a search for the article Aunt Candace had found on Winona's dispute with Haylee under her old pen name. "She definitely had issues with Winona over that publisher fiasco, but she must have known she was in the wrong. I'm not sure why she'd choose now to bring it up again."

"Maybe Winona threatened to expose her," said Estelle. "I don't know, I'm just throwing out ideas here."

"Worth looking." I typed varying phrases into the search engine but found nothing new. "No idea how that accounts for Tiffany's death, though."

"Maybe Tiffany found out… but no, she already knew," said Estelle. "That's what Aunt Candace implied, anyway. But there's no proof she's connected."

"Maybe there is." I paused my scrolling on a more recent article. "Looks like Haylee was accused of cheating in another contest a few years ago."

"Really?" She peered over my shoulder as I loaded up the article. "She was caught bribing people to vote for her?"

"Apparently," I said. "Maybe that's what this was about, not the publisher fiasco."

"Good point." Estelle lifted her gaze from my phone screen. "It's more recent, but still… Winona invited her to the ceremony, and she was one of the runners-up. It doesn't make much sense for her to send Haylee an invitation if she thought her life was in danger."

"Maybe she didn't," I said. "Or... I don't know. I'm still not seeing how Tiffany fits into this."

"Maybe both of them found out the truth," she said. "Or Tiffany found out Haylee killed Winona, so Haylee retaliated... I'm definitely channelling Aunt Candace here. This is all guesswork."

"No, it's not a bad theory." But if Tiffany had learned the identity of the killer and died for it, she hadn't told anyone else in the library about her suspicions, had she?

Estelle shook her head. "Without evidence, we can't prove anything."

"Sylvester seemed to think the evidence didn't matter," I said. "The physical evidence, that is."

"Did he?" she said.

"Think outside the box," I murmured, thinking of the manuscript. "Did Aunt Candace ever offer an update on Winona's unfinished manuscript? She was busy reading it the last time I spoke to her."

"Knowing her, she'll pull an all-nighter and show up tomorrow morning with a bunch of theories," said Estelle. "As for whether they'd be relevant, though... I'm not sure we can count on it."

I rubbed my forehead. "I don't know. The Forbidden Room gave the manuscript to me as evidence, but it wasn't specific on how it linked to the killer."

"Sleep on it," she suggested. "That's what I'm doing. The answer might come to you when you least expect it."

I hope so. The case weighed heavily on my mind, but harder to forget was the fact that I might have lost my chance to keep Laney from being seduced into the vampires' contingent. Evangeline had said her choice was inevitable and that she'd always choose the vampires first, because she *was* one... but that didn't mean her choice was a foregone conclusion. She could make up her own mind, and I had to believe it was possible for her to get out of Evangeline's clutches, whichever choice she made.

For now, I had a mystery to solve.

14

I woke early the following morning, in a much better mood than yesterday. It helped that I'd slept decently, for a wonder, probably because Sylvester was too busy watching the guests to wake me up by singing in my ear or pretending to fly off with my dad's journal.

After I'd got dressed, I put the journal into my bag and went downstairs, finding that Laney still wasn't back. I hadn't expected her to be, but my heart sank all the same to think of her trapped in that creepy old church with Evangeline and the others, listening to their attempts to lure her away from me. Strong-willed as she was, she was a novice compared to the other vampires and they all knew it.

In the kitchen, I found Estelle and Aunt Adelaide had made breakfast and helped myself to a plateful of toast.

"Are you okay, Rory?" said Aunt Adelaide sympathetically.

"I told her about Laney," said Estelle.

My throat closed up. "Yeah. I guess she didn't come back, right?"

"No," said Estelle, "but it's only been a night, that's all. Not to mention the guests are still here. I don't blame her for staying away until they're gone."

"Guess it'll take some time to meet all the other vampires," I allowed, picking up a mug of coffee. "But Evangeline is persistent. Now she has her, she won't let her go easily, and if Laney feels like she needs to stay there to get some proper lessons, she might make that choice anyway."

"I'm sure she'll make the right decision," said Aunt Adelaide. "Once she's gained all the information she wants to from Evangeline."

"You think she's using this as an opportunity to satisfy her own curiosity rather than actually joining the other vampires?" I asked.

"Absolutely," said Estelle.

"It's understandable," said Aunt Adelaide. "If I were her, I might do the same."

"I guess," I said. "It felt like Evangeline kept wearing her down by talking about how we were all keeping her away from the vampires on purpose and that she really belongs with them, not with us. It hit a sore spot, because I *was* keeping her away from the other vampires. I thought she trusted me."

"But you said she did stand up for you against Evangeline," said Estelle.

"Yeah, she did," I said. "She stood her ground the whole time. It was pretty impressive. But what got her was the fact that Evangeline offered to teach her to read minds. To control her talents."

"I think she was doing well enough on her own," said Aunt Adelaide.

I looked down. "The problem is, she lost control and read my thoughts a couple of times, and now Evangeline wants to use that link to get at the information on the journal. She openly admitted it."

"Of course she does," said Aunt Adelaide with a scowl on her face. "I have no doubts your friend is well aware of that, though, Rory. She won't let herself be manipulated."

I hoped she was right. "On top of that, she couldn't get anything from reading Betsy's thoughts except that she's not the killer. Which disproves Aunt Candace's theory of her being out for revenge. She didn't have the chance to read Haylee's mind before she had to run out of the jail because Betsy saw her and raised the alarm, and now I doubt she'll be allowed back in. Evangeline wouldn't allow it even if Edwin would."

"Edwin is already questioning the others, I'm sure," said Aunt Adelaide. "He'll be at the library in an hour to talk to the suspects who are still here. He also mentioned there being rumours of a vampire in the jail yesterday when I spoke to him on the phone earlier. I didn't realise your friend had been there at the time, so I didn't know that was who he was talking about."

I groaned. "Great. Betsy is off the suspect list, which leaves…"

Haylee. Also, Beverly. I did need to talk to them again, but not without a plan. With Laney gone, I'd lost my mind-reading advantage as well. What had Sylvester said, though? Think outside the box… outside of the physical evidence. Whatever *that* meant.

"Haylee," said Estelle. "I reread that article yesterday

about her argument with Winona. And the other one, which mentioned her cheating in a past contest. We can ask Edwin to probe further."

"We have to solve this today if we want to open the library as normal tomorrow, though," I added. Not that the others needed to know. We were all painfully aware of the time limit. "Did the other guests get up to any mischief last night?"

"No," said Estelle. "Sylvester was keeping a close watch on them. I think he let them know it, too."

"So that's why he didn't come to wake me up," I said. "I wonder if Aunt Candace has finished reading that manuscript yet?"

"I bet she probably has," said Aunt Adelaide. "I'm going to make a start on the returns while we wait for Edwin."

"I'll help you in a bit," said Estelle.

We finished up our breakfast and went into the lobby, which was deceptively quiet. Edwin and the trolls had yet to show up, so I slipped upstairs to check up on Cass.

"Go away," she mumbled when I knocked on the door to her corridor.

"Just checking you're still alive," I said. "If you need us, we're downstairs."

As I headed for the stairs, Sylvester gave a loud hoot of laughter from behind, startling me. "Good luck with that."

I continued downstairs, with one eye on the owl flying above my head. "I heard you were watching the guests last night. You didn't terrorise them, did you?"

"Why would I do such a thing?" he said.

I gave him an eye-roll. "We both know why. Is the Forbidden Room likely to be any help today?"

"You only get one question," he said. "I'll be nice and not count *that* as a question."

"How generous of you." Below, I spotted Aunt Candace walking out of the living quarters with Winona's manuscript tucked underneath her arm. "Maybe there was a clue inside that book."

Sylvester clucked his beak. "Or maybe she just wanted to read it anyway."

He might well be right, but we were short enough on concrete evidence for me to be willing to try anything, so I reached the lobby and approached Aunt Candace. "Did you read it?"

"Yes, I did." She yawned. "I finished at five this morning. Interesting read… riveting. The details on how to hide a body were particularly meticulous. But it's unfinished."

"Anything which might point to who killed Winona?" I pressed.

She gave another yawn. "I'll have to think about it. I believe the police will be wanting this back."

"Or her family," I said. "Edwin isn't here yet. Can I take a look?"

I didn't exactly have time to read the whole thing myself, but I took the manuscript from her anyway. The thick wad of paper was unwieldy enough that it surprised me that she'd carried it all the way here. As I placed it on the desk, my gaze fell on the front page, which was imprinted with the name of the publisher. *Sunny Day Press*.

I'd seen that name before. Pulling out my phone, I checked the article and found the name of Haylee's former publisher.

"Hey, Rory," Estelle appeared behind me. "What—oh, that's Winona's manuscript. Aunt Candace finished it?"

"Look at that." I pointed to the publisher name. "That's the name of Haylee's old publisher. Why would Winona publish under that imprint, considering they stole people's money and Winona herself is one of the people who exposed them as frauds?"

"Good question," said Estelle. "I'll check and see if Winona's website mentions the name of the publisher."

As she picked up her phone, I gave the opening pages another scan, my gaze snagging on the dedication. The book was dedicated to Rylie James. I'd seen that name before, too…

Aunt Candace cleared her throat. "Is nobody going to thank me for reading through that whole book in search of evidence?"

"Aunt Candace," I said. "Do you know of someone called Rylie James?"

She blinked. "I recognise the name. Why?"

"Winona dedicated her book to this person," I said. "Not only that, she's also apparently publishing with Sunny Day Press, which also happens to be the name of Haylee's old publisher. Who *is* Rylie James?"

"Good question," said Aunt Candace, pulling out her phone and loading up the article again. "According to the footnotes on this article, she's a biographer."

"She is," said Estelle, her eyes on her own phone screen. "She was working on a book about fraud in business."

"But publishing under the name of a fraudulent publisher?" I raised a brow. "Something's weird there."

"Tell me about it." Estelle scrolled down her phone screen. "Not sure what we're missing, but..."

She trailed off, then showed me her phone screen. I loaded up the same article on my own phone, confirming they matched. As it turned out, Haylee and Winona had once been business partners, when they'd set up Sunny Day Press *together*. Back when both of them had been using different names.

That changes everything.

"Damn," said Estelle quietly. "They covered this up well."

No kidding. It looked as though Haylee had indeed stolen money from the authors *and* from her ex-business partner, and they'd parted ways as a result. Then Winona had recreated the publisher as her own imprint and taken the name for herself in order to publish a new manuscript... while dedicating said manuscript to her old pseudonym. If I were Haylee, I might be pretty ticked off at that, but did that mean Haylee had killed her?

"Why did Haylee end up being nominated for the award, then?" I asked. "Was it legitimate?"

"Maybe," said Estelle. "Or not, given her history. This looks bad for Haylee, I'd say that much."

The only way to know for sure was to talk to her again, so we'd have to wait for Edwin to show up before we could tell him about our new discoveries.

"I wish Laney had been able to read Haylee's mind as well as Betsy's yesterday," I said. "Is everyone else still in their rooms?"

"Yes," said Estelle. "We're going to bring them down in small groups to speak to Edwin in order to reduce any opportunities for potential trouble."

"All right." I returned my attention to my phone and ran another search on the publisher name. Halfway down the page, I found a link to a blog which had reviewed one of their first titles, published back when Haylee and Winona had still owned the press together. I skimmed down the screen and came to a halt.

The name attached to the blog was Beverly's.

"Beverly," I said.

"What about her?" said Estelle.

"She used to be a reviewer for Sunny Day Press's titles," I said. "Not sure if she still is, but she supported and promoted their titles on her blog."

Looked like I needed to have a word with her again after all.

"She'll be on her way downstairs with the others soon enough," said Estelle. "Ah—there's Edwin."

The elf policeman entered the library, accompanied by his troll guards, and walked over to the desk.

"Everything in order?" he said.

"More or less," said Estelle. "The guests are on their way downstairs. I'll ask my mum to start bringing them into the lobby."

Sure enough, the guests began to come down the other staircase, following Aunt Adelaide's lead. The trolls stood at the ready in case anyone tried to make a break for it, but the guests moved in an orderly procession through the Reading Corner. When I spotted Beverly, I walked into step with her. "Can I have a word?"

"Sure," she said. "Where are we going?"

"Edwin wants a word with you all," I said. "But first, I need to ask you a question about Sunny Day Press."

She blinked. "Huh?"

"You know, the publisher," I said. "You used to review their titles on your blog."

"Oh," she said. "Yeah. That."

I frowned. "You do remember, right?"

I'd never thought she was all there, but this was the first time her expression had showed no recognition whatsoever. Her blog had looked fairly active, too, and had been updated recently even though it'd been years since she'd reviewed any titles from the seemingly extinct small press.

"Is your vampire friend still around?" she asked.

"Not right now." Uh-oh. Had she figured out Laney had been reading her mind? She might be sharper than I'd thought, but that didn't explain why she was pretending not to remember the publisher Haylee had once worked for. Or maybe she wasn't pretending and had genuinely forgotten. "If you remember anything about the publisher, can you tell Edwin?"

"Everyone, come over here," said one of the trolls, and Beverly was herded into line along with the others. I extricated myself from their group to watch them leave, more perplexed than ever.

Aunt Adelaide led the guests out of the library with the trolls marching on either side of them, while I approached Edwin at the rear of their group. "Did anyone in the jail give you trouble last night?"

"No, but Betsy kicked up a fuss about an alleged break-in," he said. "She was insistent that she saw a vampire. We searched the whole jail and never found one, so I assume she was raving in the hopes of gaining sympathy."

"Um..." Nothing for it. "That was Laney. She had a

hunch about the killer's identity, and she wanted to read her mind, but Betsy spotted her. Listen—"

"Your friend?" he said in disbelieving tones. "You're telling me she broke onto our property?"

"She's with Evangeline now." We left the library and began to follow the others across the square. "She made a mistake in going into the jail, but she can read minds, and I think she might be able to use that ability to get a lead on the killer. Haylee is definitely hiding something."

"What?" he said, looking at me as though he thought I was deranged. "You can't expect me to bring a vampire into the jail after she broke in without my permission."

She's with Evangeline anyway. Who knew, maybe the culprit would confess of her own accord now we had more proof. "Okay, forget Laney for a moment. I found out that Winona's new book is going to be published under an imprint which used to belong to her and Haylee. They used to be business partners."

"What?" he said. "I fail to see what that has to do with your friend's transgressions."

"It doesn't." Maybe I should have led with that first, but I couldn't escape the feeling that my chances to get proper answers were sliding through my fingertips like grains of sand. "Haylee and Winona were business partners who used to run a publisher together, before Haylee committed fraud and ended up in trouble for it. I think that might be why Winona was killed."

The library door flew open behind us, and Aunt Candace sprinted into view, hopping down the steps and across the square. "That scoundrel."

"Who?" I waited for her to catch up with us,

wondering what on earth she was raving about. It must be important if she'd left the library.

Aunt Candace dug in the pocket of her cloak. "I found something interesting from Tiffany's correspondence."

I frowned. "Tiffany is dead."

"I know she is," she said. "But she left her phone unlocked, and I found an interesting string of messages from after the ceremony."

"Wait, you stole her phone?" I said.

"That's evidence," said Edwin. "I'm going to have to ask you to hand it in, Candace Hawthorn—"

"Look." Aunt Candace insistently thrust the phone into my face. "Winona was about to expose some pretty major secrets about certain people."

"Whose secrets?" I tried to give the messages a scan, but it was hard to focus with Aunt Candace's hand shaking with excitement "Haylee's?"

"Not just hers." Aunt Candace's voice brimmed with triumph. "Look at the name on the email."

"Rylie James," I read. "Of course. It was an alias Winona was using years ago, when she exposed Haylee's fraud of their old publisher. Guess she must have kept using the name after all."

But the messages Tiffany had been exchanging with Winona were more recent than that. "The contest. Haylee was bribing people to vote for her."

"Exactly," said Aunt Candace. "Tiffany caught onto her when she found her emailing the same people."

"Give me that phone!" Edwin spluttered.

"What are you doing?" Aunt Adelaide had noticed the ruckus, and she backtracked to join us, leaving the trolls to escort the guests the rest of the way to the police station. "Whatever that is, Candace, I'm guessing you're not supposed to have it?"

"It's Tiffany's phone," I explained. "She and Winona were exchanging correspondence about Haylee before the contest. They knew she was trying to manipulate the votes."

"She did?" said Aunt Adelaide. "Haylee hasn't confessed to anything, right?"

"We need to talk to Haylee and show her the proof so she can't deny being involved," I said. "Edwin, can we talk to her?"

He pinched the bridge of his nose. "She's next on the list to be questioned anyway, but I can't allow you to bring that vampire friend of yours with you."

"Laney isn't around," I said. "But we don't need to be able to read Haylee's thoughts. Just bring up the publisher, and this article. She won't be able to deny it."

With a resigned expression, Edwin beckoned us to follow him. "Fine, but Candace, you're not to hassle the other prisoners, is that clear?"

"I'll watch her," said Aunt Adelaide. "Really, Candace, when did you take her phone?"

"She left it lying around when I caught her inside the living quarters," said Aunt Candace. "What? It's her own fault for wandering out of bounds to begin with."

I left them to their arguments, quickening my pace until I caught up to the others outside the police station. There, the three of us waited in the reception area while Edwin and the trolls escorted the newcomers to the holding cells.

Aunt Adelaide and Aunt Candace continued to bicker

until the two trolls led Hayley out through the door and into the interrogation room at the side.

Edwin stood in the doorway and cleared his throat. "Let's get this done. Candace, Aurora, you can come in, but keep your distance and don't start any trouble. That clear?"

Aunt Candace and I both entered the room behind the elf. Haylee sat in a hard-backed metal chair in front of a table, her hands cuffed and her expression resigned.

"What're you doing here?" she asked me.

"Does the publisher name Sunny Day Press mean anything to you?" I said.

She frowned. "What of it?"

"Rhonda Mallory," said Aunt Candace. "She was your old alter ego when you ran that publisher. Don't deny it. You and Winona used to be business partners, didn't you?"

Her face paled. "I don't know what you're insinuating, but we put the matter behind us."

"Or so you wanted everyone to think," I said. "Winona took over the publisher, and I'm guessing you weren't much of a fan of that, were you?"

"She was welcome to do whatever she liked," she said.

"Except expose you for bribing people to vote for you?" said Aunt Candace. "Tiffany, too."

She sat still, her jaw set, while I pulled out the article on my phone and scrolled down to find her name listed among the people running the publisher. Not just her name, but there were several other listed staff members. I didn't recognise the names, but they might be aliases, too.

"How'd you smuggle in the poison?" I asked her.

"That's the part I'd like to know the answer to, considering Winona's the one who brought the wine."

No answer came from Haylee, who remained stubbornly silent. When I read over the names of the other staff members, an idea struck me. I ran an internet search on their names and immediately came up with a familiar picture. Alana Flower, or whatever her real name was, had been one of the staff members at the press, too.

There was more than one person involved in this scheme.

"Alana was in on this, too," I said to her. "Wasn't she?"

Haylee said nothing.

"Alana?" said Aunt Candace. "She's in the holding cells, isn't she? Let me speak to her."

"Wait!" Edwin tried to block her path, but Aunt Candace marched out of the room before he could stop her and went straight for the holding cells.

I hastened to follow her, tracking her down in front of the cell where Alana sat in a slumped position, her expression slightly dazed as though she had no idea where she was.

"Oh, hello," she said. "Something wrong?"

"Yes," said Aunt Candace. "Something is definitely wrong. Did you work at Sunny Day Press a few years ago?"

"Did I what?" she said.

"We have the proof right here." I held up my phone. "You and Haylee were both staff members at Sunny Day Press before it shut down. Did you know Winona had started to publish under that imprint again?"

"Winona?" she echoed. "No, but I cut all ties with her a long time ago."

"Except when you ended up in the running for her prize," I added. "You and Haylee were both runners-up, in fact. Did you know she was accused of bribing people to vote for her?"

"No, I didn't," she said. "That's an awful thing to say."

Her voice sounded strange. I glanced at Aunt Candance and alarm flickered inside me when she pulled out her wand.

As she pointed it at Alana, a flash of light engulfed the other witch. A second later, Beverly appeared in her place.

"What the—?" I broke off. "Beverly? Is that you?"

"If I had to guess, they swapped places using a disguise charm," said Aunt Candance in self-satisfied tones. "Beverly has been helping them from the start."

"Whoa." I looked between them, my heart sinking in my chest. "Where *is* Alana? The real one?"

"It's too late now," Beverly said. "She's probably flying up north by now."

Flying? "You helped her escape?"

"No." She looked down at her hands. "She escaped by herself. Is your vampire friend going to read my mind?"

"What does that have to do with anything?" I said.

"I didn't kill anyone." She tripped over the words. "So if she reads my mind, I'm innocent. You know I am."

"Beverly, you've committed a crime, too," said Edwin. "Where is Alana?"

Gone. If she'd taken flight, how were any of us supposed to catch her? I couldn't ride a broomstick yet, while my biblio-witch magic didn't work well away from the library. Yet if she got far enough away, she'd be able to take on a new pen name and hide within another magical community without ever being found out.

The image of a vampire's speed came to mind, and a sense of steely resolve filled me. If we didn't catch Alana, we'd never bring her to justice. Unless we had help from someone who could catch her no matter how far she ran.

I needed Laney's help, even if it meant antagonising Evangeline again.

15

Aunt Candace and I walked back out into the reception area, followed by a perplexed Edwin. "Alana is the killer? Are you sure Beverly was telling the truth?"

"No, since we can't read her mind." One person could, of course, but that wasn't the important thing here. "Alana left town and told Beverly to take her place, using a spell to disguise herself so we'd think she was Alana. She used to work at Haylee's publisher, while Beverly was a reviewer for them. They're all in this together."

"You need to work on your security spells," added Aunt Candace. "Fancy not noticing they swapped places."

"You didn't notice at first either," I reminded her.

"But why *did* they swap places?" Edwin said.

"I think she and Beverly initially swapped places so if I brought Laney in here to read their minds, Alana would seem to be innocent," I explained. "And she's already read Beverly's mind once already. I assume that means Alana committed the murder, but she must have had a lot of faith in Beverly not to give the game away."

That, or Alana had had every intention of disappearing as soon as she left town. With the number of alter egos she and her allies had already used, this probably wasn't the first time she'd vanished and started afresh as a new person.

"Hang on," said Edwin. "Alana is the one who poisoned Winona and Tiffany? Am I hearing this right?"

"Haylee and Alana conspired to commit murder together," I said. "I'm guessing it was Alana who actually did it. Haylee must have thought she was a good enough actress not to let anything slip."

I'd bet they hadn't accounted for a vampire being present in the library when they'd concocted their scheme, but in every other part of their plan, they'd succeeded. They'd smuggled in the poison and disposed of the evidence while avoiding detection.

Edwin's shoulders slumped. "Can you explain why Haylee was given an award, then? She claims it proves she can't be the killer."

"Haylee bribed people into voting for her in the contest," I said. "I don't know why Winona gave her the award anyway. Maybe she didn't yet have proof."

"She didn't," said Aunt Candace. "The messages I saw on Tiffany's phone prove that. But she and Tiffany have suspected Haylee of being up to her old antics for a long time. It's possible they wanted to use this event to catch her in the act. She's a slippery one."

I returned to Haylee's interrogation room, where she sat with a belligerent expression on her face. "You never explained why your perfume showed up all over the crime scene."

"I was framed," she said.

"Forgive me if I don't believe a word you say," said Aunt Candace, entering the room behind me. "Where's Alana taken off to, then?"

"I have no idea, but I doubt you'll catch her," said Haylee. "She's probably miles away by now."

Perhaps, but with his swift Reaper speed, Xavier might be able to catch up to her, assuming he could get away from his boss. I shot him a message, but the odds of him being able to sneak away from the Grim Reaper and leave town were lower than the odds of Laney escaping Evangeline. If anyone could chase Alana down, it was Laney, and this situation surely counted as urgent enough for Evangeline to make an exception, right? Besides, it wasn't like she had Laney under her wing forever. She was just teaching her a few tricks, nothing more.

"If I were you, I'd go back to the library," said Edwin. "You too, Candace."

"C'mon," I told her. "I have an idea."

"This I'd like to hear." Aunt Candace walked with me outside the police station. "If it involves flying on one of Cass's creatures, though, I'll have to decline."

"No, I'm going to ask Laney to chase Alana," I said. "I bet she can catch up to her."

"Of course she can," she said. "You'd better hope the vampires listen to you, Rory."

"Can you tell Estelle and Aunt Adelaide about what happened back there with Beverly and Alana?" I asked. "I'll be back before you know it. Oh—and you know those other staff members listed as working for Sunny Day

Press? I bet some of them are still out there under other aliases, too."

"Precisely my thinking," she said. "We'll hunt them down. I'll tell Adelaide. You work your powers of persuasion on Evangeline."

I didn't feel very persuasive, but when Xavier's response came through telling me the Grim Reaper had seen through his attempts to sneak out and find me, I knew it would be my last chance. I walked to the church where the vampires spent their time, my nerves building with each step. While most of them slept during the day, I had little doubt Evangeline would be expecting me to return and beg on Laney's behalf.

Here's hoping she was in a generous mood.

When I knocked, a male vampire I didn't know answered the door. "Aurora Hawthorn. Evangeline said you might show up to collect your friend."

"I'm not here to collect her," I said. "I found the culprit who committed two murders and she flew out of town. I need Laney's help to chase her down before she gets out of range and disappears."

Evangeline glided into view, wearing a stunning black dress that matched her waterfall of hair. "Come to beg me to allow you to see your friend, have you?"

"No, I've come to politely ask for Laney's help in chasing down a killer."

"I see," she said "My answer is no."

"I thought it was Laney's choice," I said. "You let her decide whether to stay with you or not—"

"And she chose to stay here with me," she said. "She has yet to decide otherwise."

"This isn't—" I broke off at an alarming screeching

noise, as Sylvester swooped overhead, away from the library and off into the overcast sky.

"It looks to me like your family is already on top of things," she remarked. "Good day."

The second vampire slammed the door in my face without a word. I debated knocking again and pressuring her to hear me out, but we'd wasted enough time already. With a curse, I spun on my heel and ran back downhill, towards the town square. When I opened the door to the library, I heard Cass shouting at full volume from the direction of the stairs while Estelle stood near the desk.

"What happened?" I asked Estelle.

"Someone took the wraith," she replied.

"What?" I stared at her. "How?"

"I have no idea," she said. "Cass is furious, though. Laney didn't leave the door open again, did she?"

"She can't have. She wasn't even here." Was this part of Beverly and Haylee's plan? Or had Alana come back after all? "Did Aunt Candace tell you that Alana is the killer and she and Beverly swapped places so Alana could sneak out of town? She must have taken the wraith with her."

"More like she bribed Beverly into helping her escape," said Aunt Candace, emerging from behind a shelf. "She's certainly resourceful. I can turn up all kinds of information if I search her aliases."

"You don't have time to search her aliases, Candace," said Estelle. "We need to get that creature back. It's never been outside the library, and I don't know what we'll do if it finds its way into a normal community and starts attacking people."

"Not only that, Evangeline won't let Laney help us chase Alana down and catch her," I said. "Can we use a tracking spell or something? I saw Sylvester flying out of town, but I don't know that he'll be able to catch her."

"A tracking spell takes two days to brew. There's no time." Estelle pulled out her Biblio-Witch Inventory. "We can hop to the next town over with the travel spell, but that's not precise enough…"

"Might have to do." I pulled out my own Biblio-Witch Inventory. "We can keep hopping around until we find her. It's inefficient, but I can't think of any other way. With luck, we'll spot her on a broomstick somewhere north of town."

Cass marched into view. "That's it. I'm going after her."

"Wait," said Estelle, but her sister was already pulling out her own Biblio-Witch Inventory. Cass flipped open the book and pressed her fingertip to the page, and in a flash of light, she disappeared.

"Should have seen that one coming." I looked away from the spot where she'd vanished. "Can she handle Alana *and* the wraith at the same time?"

"You should stay here and watch the library," Aunt Adelaide told us. "I'll go after her."

"One of us ought to stay with Edwin," I said. "I wouldn't put it past Haylee and Beverly to have something else cooked up to make sure they get away without punishment. And there are the other staff members from Haylee's old publisher to find, too. They might've been hidden among the other guests."

"Very well," said Aunt Adelaide. "Candace, you stay here. Rory… are you sure you want to go after Alana?"

"I'm sure." I wanted to help my family, and besides, I was the one who'd got Laney stuck under Evangeline's watch at a time when we needed her help. It was also hard to forget that if she'd read Haylee's thoughts, we might have managed to solve this case much sooner.

"I'll go with you, Rory." Estelle held up her Biblio-Witch Inventory. "Ready?"

"Sure." I called Jet over to me. "Jet, can you fly up north of the town and look for a witch on a broomstick flying away from Ivory Beach? We're tracking a killer. Sylvester is, too, so keep an eye out for him."

"Of course, partner!"

He swooped out of the library through the open window. Meanwhile, I pictured the fields I knew lay north of Ivory Beach, opened my Biblio-Witch Inventory, and tapped the word *travel*.

Estelle and I both vanished in the same instant. In another, the library was replaced by open fields. A nice view, but I didn't recognise my surroundings at all, and Estelle was nowhere nearby. Oh, no. We'd ended up in different places.

I trapped the word *travel* again and reappeared at the end of the same field. This way of travelling was awkward, but quicker than running on foot. I couldn't see Estelle *or* Cass, though my heart lifted with relief when I spotted the dark shape of Jet flying over the fields.

"Hey, Jet," I called. "Can you see her?"

"Over there, partner!" he squeaked, his voice a faint shrillness on the breeze.

I ran to the edge of the field and spotted the dark shape of a figure on a broomstick in the distance. Knocking Alana off her broom might cause too much damage before she could confess, but unless she landed, we'd have a job and a half getting her behind bars where she belonged. We had to find a way to slow her down. I spotted Estelle some way off in the field ahead of me and ran to catch her up.

"Where's Cass?" I breathed.

"Chasing the wraith," she responded, her wand in her hand. "She hasn't found it yet, but she wants to get it back to the library before anything else. That's her priority."

"Should've known."

That left the two of us to handle Alana. I pointed my wand at her distant figure and attempted a freeze-frame spell, which missed. Estelle's spell missed, too, and we ran closer, trying to catch up to her from underneath.

A flash of light came from behind us and another red-haired figure appeared in the middle of the field, her wand in her hand and her cloak billowing behind her.

"Get back here!" yelled Aunt Candace. "This is for Tiffany!"

"What is she doing?" I said to Estelle.

She must have come for revenge for her ex-cowriter's sake. As we gawped at her, Aunt Candace overtook Estelle and me and fired off a spell. At once, Alana's broom shot in the wrong direction and began to spin. Alana screamed, hanging off the broom by her fingertips, and then her grip broke and she tumbled head over heels towards the ground. Before she landed, however, Alana waved her wand and slowed her descent, landing on her feet. When she faced us, her hair was wind-swept and her eyes wild.

"What do you people want with me?" she demanded.

"You murdered two people," I said to her. "You killed Tiffany because she was going to expose how you poisoned Winona, which you did to stop her from investigating how Haylee bribed people to vote for her in the award. The pair of you both worked for the same publisher, before it was shut down for fraud. Is that right?"

"You're lying," she said. "You can't prove it."

"We have the proof, and so do the police," Aunt Candace. "Beverly is already in custody and so is Haylee. I don't think it was very nice of you to leave them to take the blame, but this isn't the first time you've used murder to get your way, is it? I found some interesting stories about your deceased ex-husband, for one, spurred by what I read in Winona's manuscript."

Whoa. If it was true, no wonder Alana had been so quick to volunteer to be the one to commit murder.

Alana's expression flattened, and she held up her wand, waving it in a complex motion I didn't recognise. Estelle cast a shielding spell, as did I, and the spell fizzled out before it could make contact with any of us.

Then a blast of air hit both of us from behind. My wand flew from my hand and I tumbled head over heels, catching my balance in time to see someone else running uphill. *Haylee.* She waved her wand again, this time sending Aunt Candace tumbling in mid-air.

"How did you get out of jail?" Aunt Candace caught her balance, but she'd dropped her wand, too.

I pushed upright and got to my feet, but my wand had vanished somewhere in the grass and both Alana and Haylee were armed while the rest of us weren't. The battle suddenly looked decidedly one-sided.

Worse, a familiar shadow swept in behind Haylee. The wraith slithered across the grass, following her lead, shadows creeping through the field.

"Thanks for loaning me this creature," Haylee said to us. "And for leaving that cage lying around. I doubt

Beverly would have been able to smuggle it out of the library otherwise."

"Beverly did that?" She was sneakier than I'd given her credit for, though she and Alana had done something similar with their face-swapping trick. "How'd you get it to follow you here?"

"Your elf policeman ought to have put the same spell on the jail as the one you used on the library which prevented us from getting out," she said. "It was easy to transport both of us out of there after its escape distracted everyone for long enough for me to get out of my handcuffs."

Damn. It was a good job Estelle and I had bound the library so that nobody could use magic to get out, because if we hadn't, Haylee would probably have already done a runner a long time ago. So would Alana and Beverly, while our attention was too focused on Betsy Blake to consider whether there was more than one person involved in the two murders.

On the other hand, we hadn't foreseen the wraith getting captured either, while all three of us had ended up divested of our wands.

I kept an eye on Haylee and the others as I took a step forwards, my other eye searching the grass for my missing wand. "You still left Beverly behind?"

"She was happy to stay in jail to make sure we got away safely," said Haylee.

"That's nice." Beverly had been willing to do anything for the authors she hero-worshipped, apparently even capture a book wraith and set it loose in the police station to help Haylee get out of her cuffs. And Haylee had repaid her by leaving her to suffer the punishment on her behalf.

"Get away from that wraith!" Cass waved her wand and fired off a quick spell at Haylee. Haylee spun on the spot and deflected the spell with a wave of her own wand.

"You should have stayed in the library," Haylee told her. "I wonder if book wraiths like the taste of bibliowitches as much as they like ancient texts?"

My heart sank as the creature's creeping tentacles inched closer and closer. Not only did we not have our wands—except for Cass, and I suspected she'd never attack a magical creature even in her own defence—we didn't have any means of returning the beast to its cage, either. The wraith oozed around Haylee, its shadowy tentacles inching across the grass.

Then it struck. I cringed, startling when my wand flew into the air, propelled by a shadowy tendril which pushed it into my hand. Two more threads of shadow handed Estelle's and Aunt Candace their wands back, too, and both of them looked equally startled.

Cass let out an unexpected laugh. "You didn't think it'd attack us, did you? The creature lives in the library. It trusts us more than it trusts you, I guarantee it."

It's helping us. Not attacking us at all. As Haylee and Alana stared at the wraith, Cass raised her wand and blasted both of them off their feet. I raised my own wand and cast a freeze-frame spell on both the witches before they could recover, while Estelle conjured up a rope.

"Help me restrain them!" she called over her shoulder to Aunt Candace, who moved in to help her tie Haylee and Alana's wrists and ankles together in order to prevent them from running off when the freeze-frame spell ran out.

As for me, I approached Cass. "Did you know that was going to happen?"

"Of course I did," she said. "They made a mistake targeting the book wraith. I knew it'd take our side."

"You'll both spend a long time in jail where you can have a good think about what you've done," Aunt Candace told the two restrained witches. "Without using a spell to get out this time."

Haylee screamed incoherently. "I shouldn't be here. This is a mistake. A mistake—"

Aunt Candace flicked her wand, casting a spell which silenced her in an instant. Meanwhile, Sylvester flew down from the sky and plucked both witches' wands from the grass with a menacing caw. Both witches sagged onto the grass in defeated silence.

"That's that taken care of, then," Aunt Candace said in a satisfied tone. "We just need to get those two into jail and we're done."

I frowned. "How are we going to get the wraith back to the library, then?"

"Leave that to me," said Cass.

16

We used magic to travel back to the library, landing in the lobby with our two captives trussed up behind us. Aunt Adelaide was on the phone when we landed. She glanced at us once and said, "Edwin, come here to the library. We have Haylee *and* Alana restrained." She hung up the phone before the elf could ask any more questions. "I don't remember telling you to go chasing after the others, Candace."

"I wasn't about to let those two get away with what they did to Tiffany," she said.

Haylee tried to headbutt her in the legs, but missed, her mouth open in a silent howl. As Aunt Adelaide moved towards the captives, Cass appeared in the lobby with the wraith wrapped around her shoulders.

Aunt Adelaide let out a startled noise at the sight of her. "What are you doing?"

"Don't worry, the wraith is loyal to us and the library," she said. "Also, it wants to move into the ancient languages section downstairs. I think it wants a change of scenery, so I'll drop it off in there. That okay?"

She shuffled away, wraith and all, without waiting for an answer.

Aunt Adelaide shook her head. "We can talk about that later, but really—"

The library door flew open and Edwin's troll guards walked in, followed by Xavier of all people.

"I managed to get away from the boss, but it took a while," he said to me. "What's going on?"

"We caught them." I stepped aside to let the trolls take the two prisoners away, and then hugged Xavier. "Let me guess... the Grim Reaper didn't see chasing after magical criminals as a good enough reason for you to shirk your duty."

"I did give you that stone to call for my help," he reminded me.

I pressed my hand to my forehead. Of course he'd given me a stone by which I could call him from anywhere and he'd be able to immediately appear at my side, but it'd slipped my mind. Besides, it wasn't as though my life had been in danger. "I forgot."

"Don't worry," he said. "It looks like your family had the situation in hand."

"They did." Even Cass, though she didn't stick around to chat with the rest of us once she'd dropped the wraith off in its new home. I needed to make a note of that one, otherwise I'd get a nasty shock the next time I went looking for something in the ancient languages section.

With the guests finally gone, we set about returning the library to its former state while I filled Xavier in on everything he'd missed, including Alana and Beverly's face-swapping spell and Haylee's scheming.

He let out a low whistle when I brought up how Beverly had captured the wraith. "Good job Cass was there. The situation might've gone badly if the wraith hadn't ended up acting on your side."

"Cass seemed confident it's too attached to the library to turn against us," I said. "Doesn't mean I'm not sceptical about her turning it loose downstairs, mind. I know it likes feeding on ancient languages, but I know I'm going to forget it's in there and get scared half to death when it next shows up."

"Maybe stick a warning sign on the door so you don't get taken off guard," he suggested.

"Sylvester will probably remove it if I do."

The owl himself was nowhere to be seen. There wasn't much he could have done to retrieve our runaway criminals or the wraith, but no doubt his pride would have taken a hit. It wouldn't have killed him to be a little more specific with the Book of Questions, but even the Forbidden Room had its limits. It wasn't like any of us had known there was more than one criminal hidden among our guests.

I wouldn't lie, it was nice to have our quiet library back again. Relatively quiet, anyway. The book wraith would cause some hair-raising encounters if it decided to stay on the ground floor, but compared to the guests which had been here all weekend, that would be simple enough to deal with.

According to Edwin, Haylee, Alana and Beverly were set to go on trial the following day. While the others had been released from custody, a fair few of them had opted to stay in town to see Winona and Tiffany's killers to get the justice they deserved. Or use the trials as novel inspiration. One or the other.

"They're going to elect a new committee to the Merry Mysteries prize and run another contest so that nobody can cheat this time," Aunt Candace said the following morning. "Maybe I'll win this time."

"Are you sure you want to get involved, considering what happened to the winners of the last one?" said Aunt Adelaide.

"I think it'll keep life interesting." She grabbed a piece of toast. "I'm working on a book based on this, too."

"Already?" said Estelle.

"Yes, I thought it was best to get on with it while it's fresh in my mind." Aunt Candace drained her coffee.

"Sure the others aren't planning the exact same?" I said.

"Even if they are, I have a unique perspective," said Aunt Candace. "Betsy will wait until I'm done before copying me, I don't doubt."

"Some things never change," Estelle murmured.

I grinned. Our family was well and truly back to normal.

That just left one worry on my mind... Laney. She hadn't come back to the library yet, nor had she sent me an update on how she was getting on with the other vampires. Understandably, she had a lot to learn, but I still worried that she'd made a firm decision and picked the other vampires over us. Despite my worries, Estelle maintained that she'd be back any day now, so I did my best to put it out of mind. Over the next few days, life returned to normal. I hung out with my family. I went on dates with Xavier. The murderers' trials came and went, and while I'd wondered if Evangeline would choose to show up and taunt me again about Laney's useful mind-reading skills, neither of them showed their faces at all.

Three days after the trial, I sat working on the front desk, and when Laney strode in with swift and silent vampire steps, I dropped my pen. "Laney."

"Hey, Rory." She gave a wan smile.

"Are you okay?" I asked.

"Of course I am," she said. "If Evangeline had tried to hurt or threaten me—or you, or your family—I would have been out of there in a second."

"I know," I said, "but I worried that she was manipulating you or forcing you to join her team. We never established whether she was one of the Founders, either."

"Yeah, I don't know about that part," she said. "I can't read *her* mind."

"I don't think anyone can," I said.

"I know how to control the mind-reading now," she added. "I should be able to get back to interacting with people normally soon enough."

"You learned that fast?"

"We came to an agreement," she said. "I'll be joining night classes at the academy with the rest of the local vampires so I can become proficient in the right skills, but I won't be living with them."

"Where will you live, then?" I asked.

"I don't know," she said. "If I had money, I'd get my own place, but I don't feel like accepting charity from the vampires. I don't trust them."

"You aren't going to go back home?" I said. "I mean—I

know you can't leave the magical world, and you're welcome to stay in the library, but—"

Surprise flickered across her face. "Your family doesn't mind?"

"Of course you can stay in the library," I said. "That was never in doubt. Even if we do attract trouble."

"I thought I was the cause of all the trouble," she said. "I mean, with the wraith, and the mind-reading and everything."

"Believe me, you're the least troublesome out of the lot of us," I said, earning a grin. "Look at Cass and Aunt Candace. Not to mention our familiars... and that's not counting the people who *visit* the library."

"I guess," she said. "Are you sure?"

"You can move back in whenever you like," I said. "Believe me. It's fine with us."

"But... the mind-reading," she said. "Your dad's journal. Evangeline wants it, and... and I can't stop her from reading *my* mind."

"I know," I said, "but I've spent long enough worrying about what's in the journal. I want to know the truth. And if Evangeline finds out as well, then at least she won't be able to taunt me any longer."

Whatever my dad had wanted to keep secret, I could only deal with it when I knew what I was up against. Then if the Founders wanted to come after me, at least I'd be prepared. It was always better to know the truth than to live in fear of it. I should know that by now.

"Okay," said Laney. "I'm in."

A smile stole onto my mouth. Evangeline hadn't won. The vampires hadn't claimed my best friend. She might have a lot to learn about the magical world, but so did I. We could learn together.

As for the Founders? If they showed their faces in town again, we'd be ready.

ABOUT THE AUTHOR

Elle Adams lives in the middle of England, where she spends most of her time reading an ever-growing mountain of books, planning her next adventure, or writing. Elle's books are humorous mysteries with a paranormal twist, packed with magical mayhem.

She also writes urban and contemporary fantasy novels as Emma L. Adams.

Find out more about Elle's books at: https://www.elleadamsauthor.com/

Find Elle on Facebook at https://www.facebook.com/pg/ElleAdamsAuthor/

Made in the USA
Monee, IL
04 May 2025